This book is dedicated to my mother, Lil Matchan, who was its inspiration.

Long in the Sleuth

A Tension on a Pension Mystery

CAROL NOVIS

Cover design: Sara Israel

Print Formatting: By Your Side Self-Publishing
www.ByYourSideSelfPub.com

Website: **carolnovis.com**

Facebook: **www.facebook.com/sleuthcozymystery**

ACKNOWLEDGMENTS

Many thanks for their unstinting encouragement and help to my family—Ben, Nurit, Avi, Max, Romain, Daniella and Tamara, and to my sisters, Judy and Linda.

Thanks also to Judy Gerstel, Tami Lehman-Wilzig, Anne Kleinberg and Judy Labensohn.

☙ Chapter One ❧

"Ouch. Take it easy, Bernice," I said, rubbing my shin. "You almost tripped me."

Bernice Baum, in neon green yoga outfit and Nikes—the better to get to the food fast—pushed me aside with her cane as she made for our table of four. For a woman with memory problems, she certainly had no difficulty remembering where the food was.

"Talk to the wall," as my late mother used to say. Bernice paid no attention to me. She shuffled to her usual seat and plunked herself down.

It was 11:30 am—lunchtime at the Melvin and Sarah Witberg Memorial Menorah Retirement Residence in Aurora, Minnesota. The elegant dining room, with its crystal chandelier, white starched napery, menu cards and thick beige carpet (so as to prevent a fall), echoed with the buzz and chatter of some 200, give or take, senior citizens. A window, stretching the full length of one wall, revealed an acre of surrounding land, with artfully scattered paths, benches and statuary. In summer, this was a well-manicured garden, but right now, it was covered by a thick blanket of Minnesota snow.

I had been living at the Menorah for almost a year now, and the scene in the dining room seemed very much as usual. How was I to know that this particular lunch would set in motion a set of circumstances that would result in me, Ellie Shapiro, in my so-called golden years, becoming involved in murder and almost giving my son Josh a heart attack?

But I'm getting ahead of myself.

The crowd had started milling around the dining room entrance at about 11. That was because lunch was a highlight of the day. (Breakfast and dinner were the other two highlights.) Residents started parking their walkers a good half hour before the doors opened, eager for Maurice, the 30-ish year old maitre d', to let us in.

Not that we were particularly hungry; we'd enjoyed the abundant breakfast buffet just a few hours ago. Bagels, lox, blintzes, hash browns, Israeli tomato and cucumber salad, French toast made with fresh challah... anything you could want. The food and the way it was served was one reason the Menorah was the place to be if you could afford it and couldn't manage anymore on your own. You could even order breakfast in bed, delivered on a tray with flowers, just like at the fancy hotels.

No, what the residents of the Menorah were hungry for at lunch time was the socializing and gossip that was served up along with the brisket, pickles and knishes at tables where you were seated with your assigned meal mates.

In short, the dining room was where the action took place.

At our table, Pearl Green, the resident prima donna, gave Bernice a disdainful look.

"*Some* people just can't wait to eat," she said, with disgust. Bernice didn't seem to mind. She not only tolerated Pearl's scorn, but followed her everywhere. I suspected Pearl actually liked being held in such awe, even if it was only by muddled Bernice.

Carefully made up, with her blond hair impeccably styled as usual, Pearl sat opposite Riva Mannheim, a dignified, grey-haired woman in her mid 80s with a slight European accent, who ignored her. Riva's habitual air of distain, though, said everything.

Riva didn't seem to enjoy the company of anyone at all, other than her small, noisy Jack Russell terrier, Schultz. (Maybe she enjoyed the company of her only daughter, but we had no way of knowing; her daughter lived in Israel.) She had coolly rebuffed every effort on my part to be friendly, making me feel like a social reject. You had the feeling that she would prefer to be called "Mrs. Mannheim" rather than by her first name, but this was Minnesota,

2

after all, not Berlin, so "Riva" it was. She was lucky it wasn't "Dahling."

The fourth one at the table was me.

And who am I?

Well, I'm in my 70s, though exactly how far into my 70s I'm not't revealing. Let's just say my AARP membership is longstanding. My face has the odd bag and line here and there, but on the whole I didn't look too terrible. I have all my teeth and hair and plenty of energy. I'm healthy, except for asthma, which with the help of my trusty inhaler seems to be well controlled. Moreover, I can still fit into a size 16. Well, an 18... but without an elastic waist, I'll have you know. (What can I tell you? I like to eat.)

In particular, I took a great interest in the doings of others. Some people called that being nosy (the nerve); I preferred to call it joie de vivre. My philosophy in life is that you can laugh or you can cry. I prefer to laugh. Of course, good food helps too.

Now Maurice served the first course, chopped liver.

At the next table, our neighbors, three women and Sam Levin, were discussing their ailments, real and imagined, loudly enough to be easily overheard by us and by anyone else nearby.

"My eyes seemed a bit yellow this morning," said Joyce Kramer, in a worried tone. "I wonder what that means."

"Maybe you have jaundice," Sadie Diamond offered eagerly. "Or liver cancer. Marla Sacks had liver cancer and her eyes turned yellow. It was terrible."

She sighed. "Marla lasted only a month, screaming in pain."

Joyce hastily pulled out a compact to examine her eyes again.

It was uncanny. The diseases they came up with always seemed to be related to what we were having for lunch, as if the menu had been specifically planned to make me lose my appetite. And it took a lot to make me lose my appetite!

Sam, who took full advantage of being one of the few males among many women, spoke up. "Now, I have no medical problems. In fact, I'm better than ever, in a lot of ways," he leered, patting his full head of slick black hair. "If you know what I mean."

Just in case we didn't, he told us. "I know how to make a woman happy."

Jeez, I thought. Sam in bed. The stuff of nightmares.

At our table, Pearl leaned in closer, and stage-whispered, "I heard that Sam is having an affair with someone here."

Bernice's eyes lit up. "With who?"

"Nobody, Bernice," I said. "People just like to make things up. It's like that joke: Mrs. Smith says to Mrs. Jones, 'I have a secret. I'm having an affair.' Mrs. Jones answers, 'Really? Who's catering?'"

The joke fell with a thud. Pearl ignored it, Bernice looked blank and Riva said nothing. She nodded, as if that just confirmed her opinion of the gossip-hungry, low-life ignoramuses around here.

Bernice got up to go the restroom, stumbled past Sam's table, pulled herself up with the aid of the tablecloth and headed off in the general direction of the door.

"Never mind Sam." Pearl was onto another topic. "I heard that there's a good-looking guy volunteering in the Community Archive. And he's not married."

I pretended to be fascinated by the roast chicken now being served. But Pearl was shrewd.

"You visited the Community Archive last week, Ellie," she pointed out. "I heard you spent a lot of time reading stuff there. I can't believe you're so interested in genealogy. It must be the new guy, right?"

Fortunately, before I could think up an evasive answer, Pearl, in drama queen mode, had suddenly decided that the food wasn't up to her exacting standards. She poked the chicken with a fork and grimaced.

"This chicken is inedible!" she intoned, waving away invisible crumbs. "Take it away! I'll have the brisket and knishes instead. I hope they're better than this garbage."

I squirmed in my red plush upholstered chair and pretended to be somewhere else. This was so embarrassing! Pearl had worked up a full head of steam and was lambasting the long-suffering maitre d', Maurice.

"For heaven's sakes, Pearl, keep your voice down," I whispered. But it was hopeless trying to stop her. Pearl was enjoying herself. She now turned her attention to me, as if instructing a lesser being.

"You can't let the staff get away with this kind of thing, Ellie," she said in a self-satisfied tone. "You have to keep them in line. We're paying enough here for proper service."

Stone-faced, Maurice removed Pearl's plate. She'd actually eaten half the so-called inedible chicken. I winked at him, hoping

4

he'd catch my meaning—"She's nuts. What can you do?"—and not take offense: He winked back. He knew.

As Maurice strode to the kitchen bearing the discarded plate, the place buzzed with shocked delight. There was nothing the residents of the Menorah Retirement Residence loved better than a scene, and here was Pearl throwing a tantrum... again. This would give the mahjong *yentas* something to talk about at today's game. There was little enough excitement around here, unless you counted Pearl's outbursts and the occasional whine of ambulance sirens.

Pearl, who was forever reminding one and all that her father had been part of the Roosevelt administration and that she had not one, but two grandsons who were doctors, as well as a granddaughter engaged to a lawyer—"an observant *Jewish* lawyer"—as she frequently reminded us—was a constant and dependable source of wicked gossip. Occasionally, the gossip was even true.

Sometimes I thought that if I had to listen to Pearl kvetching about the food, or any of the other myriad things she found to whine about, one more time, I would come right out and ask if she had forgotten her medication, and then move to another table. But changing tables was considered a social no-no because it offended people. Pearl was the burden I had to bear for moving into the Menorah Retirement Home, where meal times meant putting up with table mates you didn't get to choose.

So why, you might ask, was I here? I knew the answer only too well: because I had little choice.

When Manny had died suddenly of a heart attack, leaving poker debts I had never known about, my two grown kids had offered to help me out.

"Come stay with us," urged Tami, who lives with her husband and two children in a chaotic mess in Miami. (I love them, but no thanks.) That left my first-born, Josh, who is well into his 40s. He works in hi-tech, is ridiculously wealthy and demonstrates no signs of wanting to settle down or be burdened in any way by an elderly mother with asthma.

He showed his concern, though, by insisting that I live at the Menorah, which he pays for in full. I was grateful; it was generous of him, though I hesitated for a long time before agreeing to move in.

I finally gave in, and not only because of the asthma. Living by myself, after 55 years of marriage, was lonely. So here I was, apparently doomed to spend the rest of my life sharing a dinner table in a plush retirement home with two women who drove me nuts, and one who clearly thought me not worth bothering about.

Good thing I liked to eat.

❧ Chapter Two ❧

Pearl, the scene over to her satisfaction, settled down and waited for her brisket. But Bernice was puzzled.

"Why were you so rude, Pearl?" Turning to me, she whispered hesitantly, "Pearl was rude, wasn't she, Ellie?"

"Yes, she was," I agreed. Bernice needed confirmation about just about everything. Satisfied, Bernice adjusted her plus size yoga pants and smiled vacantly.

Pearl sniffed, but didn't bother to reply. She had little time for poor, addled Bernice though she enjoyed ordering her around. She inspected her long, manicured nails, paying particular attention to the huge diamond ring her late husband, a furniture manufacturer, had provided.

Maurice appeared with a fresh plate which he deposited in front of her.

"Here you are, Mrs. Green," he said. "Brisket and knishes."

"That looks good! I'll have some too, Maurice, please," said Bernice, batting her eyelashes girlishly, as she did at every opportunity. In fact, I'd noticed that when she'd gone to the rest room a few minutes ago, she'd taken a detour via the kitchen, no doubt in hopes of flirting with him. I was a little surprised that she remembered where the kitchen was. The poor woman was so clueless that she had tried to sit down at Sam's table by mistake when she returned. I'd had to steer her back to her place.

"Bernice, leave Maurice alone. Anyone would think you were in love with him," said Pearl. Bernice blushed. Of course, she was in love with Maurice, as Pearl knew very well. So were half the women in the room. What competition did he have? He was about 50 years younger than any of the other men around, and he wasn't married.

Most of the rest of the women mooned over Sam, the only widower in the place who could still drive at night and had a full head of black hair. Was it hair dye or genetics? None of the women really cared. It was there, where hair should be and wasn't on other men his age, and that was all that mattered.

That, and his 12-year old Cadillac, which, he liked to joke, would be bar mitzvah next year.

Personally, I found Sam a bit too full of himself, and Maurice, I knew, had a boyfriend downtown. But who was I to deny anyone the thrilling joys of unrequited love?

(And if truth be told, Pearl was right: I had my secret fantasies focused around that mysterious but gorgeous guy called Hal, who volunteered in the Community Archive. He was good-looking for his age, smart and charming with silver hair—yes, real hair. Sadly, he hadn't as yet paid me the slightest attention. But a girl can dream.)

Pearl seemed to have nothing more to complain about for the moment, and was concentrating on her meal, which was actually quite good.

Truthfully, none of us really could complain about the food or about anything else either. The Menorah Retirement Residence was the best in the city and the staff members, in true mid-Western style, were generally gracious and helpful. The suites were roomy; there was a pool, gym, an internet facility and nursing staff on call around the clock. (Although why they want to keep us alive longer is beyond me. The faster we go, the faster management can sell another suite.)

The flies in the ointment were, well, us.

When people live in close proximity, whether in a college dorm or an apartment house, they will almost certainly get on one another's nerves. And here, they really, really did.

You'd think that by their eighth decade, people would have

learned to behave like adults. Uh uh. Living at the Menorah was like being in seventh grade all over again, only with cataracts and a walker. Cliques and in-groups abounded—not to mention gossips.

There were the popular girls, the mean girls (the two categories often overlapping), the socialites, the bridge fiends—and also, I had to admit, a lot of perfectly nice people. The luckiest were those who boasted a husband still alive, preferably with all his marbles. There weren't too many of those. Next were the ones with attentive offspring living nearby. But the most exalted status at the Menorah belonged to that rare and coveted individual, the eligible widower. Like Sam.

Where did I fit in? Well, I didn't really. I'm not in the mean girl category; I'm pretty cheerful and optimistic by nature and enjoy laughing at nonsense rather than getting angry.

But I wasn't one of the popular girls either, since I've never been rich or ever lived in the fancy part of town. My husband Manny wasn't a highly respectable professional. He was a salesman.

I'm not attracted by Feldenkreis or Senior Yoga or Chair Zumba, and mahjong bores me stiff. I like rock music rather than golden oldies, even though I'm what you might call a golden oldie myself. My passions—baking, enjoying food and people-watching—are rather solitary occupations. The truth is that I just hadn't found my place yet at the Menorah Residence. I know it was crazy at my age to feel like a 17-year-old who hasn't been invited to the prom, but sometimes that's just how I did feel.

That didn't mean, though, that I was ready for a rocking chair. Though my kids obviously thought I was well-meaning but helpless, I was determined to prove them wrong. My motto: I may be old; I may have asthma, but I'm still alive and kicking. And if I can nosh on a few rugelach and enjoy a good laugh from time to time, I'm not complaining. Well, not much.

Bernice, who had a healthy appetite, was now eating with relish. "These knishes are terrific."

"Hmm." Pearl had shifted her admiring glance to her armful of bracelets. "What do they know about making knishes properly?"

I grinned. "Insult the knishes and I'll take it personally."

"Did you make the knishes, Ellie?" Bernice perked up.

"I helped," I admitted. This was false modesty. Actually, I had pretty much made them all myself. I had learned to make them from my mother, who had been an immigrant from Eastern Europe. Knishes are baked, round, savory pastries filled with cheese, meat, buckwheat, or as in the ones that I had made, mashed potatoes and fried onion. They're our version of empanadas or calzones, and they always go over big at the Menorah.

"They are good," said Riva, unexpectedly. This was high praise; Riva usually had little to say at the table, giving the general impression that she thought our conversation was beneath her notice.

"Thanks," I said, pleased. "The kitchen staff asked me to help prepare something that the residents might like, and I thought of knishes."

The residents of the Menorah loved the kind of food they'd grown up on. Give them quinoa and you'd hear a collective "feh." Give them kasha or kugel or, as today, potato knishes, and they'd all dig in like famished refugees. I'd taught the chef, Tommy, how to prepare the family recipes I'd made so often that I knew by heart, and the knishes had turned out terrific.

Pearl was dubious. "Are you allowed to bake if you aren't on staff?" she asked. "Surely there are regulations for institutional catering."

Trust her to rain on my parade.

"You're right, of course, but there is a way around it. I'm allowed to help in the kitchen, provided that I'm 'advising' rather than cooking and that I'm supervised by staff," I said. "Not that I need supervision, but Ms. Robins is a stickler for rules. As it happens, Tommy gives me free reign. He knows that I love baking and you can't do much in the toaster oven they provide in our units. They think we might burn the place down if we had real ovens."

"And they may be right," said Pearl, glancing at Bernice.

"I think I'll have another knish myself," I said, glancing around for a passing waiter. But the waiters, as well as most of the diners, now seemed to be occupied with what was going on at a nearby table.

Sam Levin was exploiting his position as cock of the walk, and loudly playing the fool by juggling knishes. His admiring claque of women admirers squealed and encouraged him.

"Watch this!" Sam said, as he stood, picked up two knishes

from his plate and tossed them into the air towards the chandelier. "Voila!" he crowed, as one knish landed somewhere in the vicinity of his face. He put the remains in his mouth. Crumbs spattered on the rug near my chair, with some bits on my shoe. When I reach down to brush them away, I noticed that there was half a pill lying there among the crumbs. I picked it up, meaning to throw it away later.

Everyone was now enjoying Sam's show, particularly Sam himself. There was some clapping and a lot of laughter, though not from everybody. Riva rolled her eyes heavenwards. Bernice, her mouth hanging open, seemed transfixed. Pearl, unimpressed, said, "He's obviously treated himself to a glass of schnapps before lunch. Or two. Or three."

Then, as everyone watched in fascinated horror, Sam's face turned red, then purple. Crumbs spewed from his mouth and fell to the rug. He tottered briefly and then crumpled slowly onto the carpet.

"Is this part of the act?" Pearl asked, looking at Sam, who was lying face down, ominously still.

"I'm pretty sure it's not," I said, my heart beating quickly. Someone screamed. A waitress dropped a tray. Maurice ran and bent over Sam and began applying resuscitation. Another staffer ran for the defibrillator. The in-house nurse appeared and the noise rose in volume.

"I knew he was too old for this nonsense," I whispered. 'Now he's had a heart attack."

There was a collective intake of breath in the room as the diners waited for Maurice to tell them what was going on. It seemed to take a long time. We couldn't really see what was happening, since the nurse together with Maurice, who were trying to revive him, hid Sam from view, but from where we sat, we could see his legs. They weren't moving.

Maurice stood up, his face pale.

"I'm sorry to say that Sam has passed away. Someone call Ms. Robins."

A waitress ran out in search of our head administrator. The buzz in the room changed to a hush. Death was nothing new, unfortunately, here, but no one actually liked to be this close to it.

The meal seemed to be over. No one had any appetite for

dessert and murmuring in subdued tones, the residents began to file out into the lobby, just outside the dining room. I wrapped up a bit of brisket from my plate in a paper napkin for Riva's dog, which was waiting for her faithfully, as he always did, tied to a column in the lobby in the area where people parked their walkers.

"Here, Riva," I said, handing her the napkin. "A treat for Schultz." Schultz stood up on his hind legs, yapping in excitement.

"That's not necessary," she said stiffly. "I feed him well. Down, Schultz."

Oh, boy. Nothing was going to make this woman friendly, especially an obvious tactic like bribing her dog, who was now looking longingly at the delicious-smelling napkin. I deposited it in a nearby rubbish bin.

Schultz was a sore point with a lot of the residents, who disliked the wild little Jack Russell terrier and thought that Menorah's policy of allowing residents to keep pets, provided they were looked after properly, infringed on their comfort. The Menorah owners, on the other hand, held the view that pets were good for older people, giving them companionship, affection and enforced exercise. Also, though this was made less public, allowing animals was a selling point to entice pet owners to take up residence in the Menorah. You had to pay extra for the pets too. So, animals, so far, were welcome.

I agreed with the house policy, though I didn't have a pet myself. I enjoyed the antics of the various resident lapdogs and cats—even Joyce's loquacious parrot, which had a surprisingly spicy vocabulary.

The dog, no fool, was now trying to jump into the bin to retrieve the meat. Riva pulled at his leash, to no effect. Schulz began running in circles, yapping even louder, and entrapping two elderly ladies in his leash.

Oh lord, what had I done? Thrown off balance by Sam's death, I had inadvertently caused chaos. I dashed over and caught one of the women before she fell; then picked up Schultz to stop him jumping around, creating even more havoc. With all the excitement, I could feel an asthma attack coming on.

The disapproving murmur of the residents who had just left the dining room rose in volume, and I could see their point: a fall in a woman of our age could be a serious thing. And now maybe Riva would be forced to get rid of her beloved pet.

Outside, the whine of an approaching ambulance grew louder. We had forgotten poor Sam, lying on the dining room carpet. How could we possibly have done that? I could see from the abashed looks on people's faces that I wasn't the only one to whom that thought had occurred.

Hastily, I handed Schultz to Riva. "I'm so sorry! It was my fault for putting the meat in the bin."

"You meant well," she said.

I was surprised. Could she be human after all?

✦ Chapter Three ✦

None of the residents seemed in a hurry to return to their suites, not even Riva. A small crowd had gathered in the lobby.

"Have they taken Sam's body out yet?" asked Bernice in her usual clueless way, craning her neck to try to see what was happening in the dining room. "Shush, Bernice," I whispered, although she was saying what we were all thinking.

A death at a retirement home is always unsettling for the residents. The general feeling is sadness tempered with relief ("It wasn't me") and foreboding ("Tomorrow it might be me.") No matter how luxuriously appointed; no matter how "discerning, creative and active" the lifestyle, as the Menorah Retirement Residence brochure put it, we all knew that the arrival of a new resident to replace the one who had left told its own story. The one who had departed was now in that great retirement home in the sky.

"Sam always enjoyed being the center of attention. He went the way he would have wanted to go—quickly. Well, maybe not quite the way he wanted to go," Mollie Levine cackled.

The women around her laughed and nodded, then immediately put on solemn faces.

Mollie, whose age—93—had no influence on her insatiable curiosity about everybody, was the first to comment. That wasn't surprising, since she was also the first to know what was going on.

She spent most of her time on the sofa in the lobby, next to the fireplace with its gas-fired faux logs which flickered day and night.

The sofa on which Mollie held court had been carefully chosen. It provided the best vantage point in the whole complex for her to keep an eye on who was doing what. That was because it faced the door, so Mollie could see who came in and who went out. The reception desk and the mail boxes were on the right of the entrance; further to the right was the entrance to the office of Ms Robins, the administrator. The Vintage Cafe coffee shop, a secondary center for gossip and the venue for bridge and mahjong games, was located to the left of the lobby. A staircase and elevator at the back of the entrance hall led up to the mezzanine, another prime viewing area.

Nobody disputed Mollie's right to the sofa. In return, she happily shared her findings with all and sundry. Were you curious about whose grandchildren visited, and whose didn't? Who was invited out for Friday night Sabbath dinner, and who wasn't? Who got real mail and who just got catalogs? Well, sit right down here beside Mollie.

Needless to say, Mollie was popular.

You couldn't dislike her though, because much as she loved gossip, she was never mean or malicious. She delighted in other people's good news and commiserated with the unfortunate, usually at great length.

Mollie was fun to look at too. In a retirement home full of grey wrens, Mollie was a peacock—bright and upbeat. No bland pastels for this lady; she read the tabloids avidly and wore whatever she thought was in fashion. Short skirts—bring them on. Tottery high heels—no problem! Hawaiian muu muus—you bet. She never appeared without full makeup, more or less accurately applied, and her hair was henna-ed an eye-popping burgundy. I admired her spirit.

Now, she had plenty to speculate about.

"I didn't know that Sam had a heart condition. It looked like it might have been something he ate. He fell down after he ate a knish. Didn't you make those knishes, Ellie?"

"The knishes were perfectly fine. I ate one myself," I said tartly. "So did you."

"You're right, I did. And now I have such an ache in my

kishkes!" That was Joyce putting in her two cents worth. She clutched her belly for effect.

Other women were starting to look alarmed. Joyce, who no doubt now thought she had food poisoning as well as liver cancer and jaundice, cried, "I feel sick." Exit left, pursued by... Oh good grief. Schultz was free of his leash again and was joining in what he clearly thought was a fun game of tag.

This was getting old. Once again, I took up the chase. But Schultz was wise to me. He darted right, then left, yapping wildly. I zigged. He zagged. I zagged. He zigged. My back went into spasm and I swear the dog was laughing at me. People were racing their walkers in their haste to escape before they could be tripped up. Those with new knees were speed walking. And now, two ambulance men, carrying a blanket-covered figure on a stretcher, were leaving the dining room.

Everyone stopped dead, so to speak. There was a collective "Oy."

"Is that Sam, Ellie?" asked Bernice.

"Yes, of course it's Sam! Who else would it be?" said Mollie. "Keep the dog away!"

No, please, no. Don't jump on him, Schultz, I thought, too paralyzed with horror to move. But Schultz was now eying this interesting new object and hopping up on his hind legs, trying to see what was on the stretcher.

"Get him off," shouted one of the ambulance men.

"Schultz!" said Riva. She glared at him. "Come here."

The dog, his tail down, knew authority when he heard it. He slunk over to Riva, who attached his leash to the handlebar of her walker.

"It's a *shandeh*, a disgrace," Joyce muttered, not quite under her breath, making sure that Riva, who was now heading out of the lobby with Schultz, could hear. "That Jack Daniels terrier dog is going to injure someone one day. I'm going to speak to Ms. Robins."

"Jack Russell, not Jack Daniels," I said. "Jack Daniels is a whiskey."

The audience ignored me, except for Joyce.

"The dog drinks whiskey? That's even worse!" she said, shaking her head. "He's drunk!"

"No," I said wearily. "He doesn't drink whiskey. It's just... oh, never mind."

"Let's not get off the point. The dog is a disgrace," said Pearl. "And just after someone has died. Where's the respect?"

Everyone immediately put on a solemn face again.

"That dog has to go. And Riva can go with it. She doesn't fit in—she doesn't even want to fit in. She thinks she's too good for us."

That was rich, coming from Pearl, the snob in diamonds, whose granddaughter, as she was forever telling us, was engaged to a religious Jewish lawyer.

It was probably hopeless, but I had to give it a try. I was never one to go along with the crowd. You might say, like the dog, I generally zigged when everyone else zagged. Anyway, there was something about Riva I liked, maybe because she also went her own way and thumbed her nose at the rest. Also, I knew something about her past that she hadn't made public, which made me particularly sympathetic to her.

"You can't tell Ms. Robins that Riva has to leave here. Maybe she has nowhere else to go. Maybe she's shy."

It was a little farfetched, and not surprisingly, my plea fell flat.

"She definitely has to go," Pearl repeated. There were nods of agreement all around.

Not if I can help it, I vowed.

"What is going on?" The icy tone stopped us in our tracks.

Ms. Justine Robins, the head administrator of the Menorah Residence, had appeared, bringing the chatter to an abrupt halt. You might think that since we were the paying customers and she was the hired help, she would be conciliatory. You would be wrong.

She ran the Menorah with the authority of the warden of a maximum security prison and even the most recalcitrant resident was wary of her.

Her voice was piercing; her manner peremptory (though sugary sweet when speaking to a potential new resident.) She wore crisp suits, never pants, and her artfully highlighted auburn hair looked like a rigid construction of acrylic. The joke was that she glued it into place every day.

I suspected that her trim *tuches* was encased in "shapewear," which was what in my day we called a girdle. If you pinched her bottom, you'd probably break a nail. (Not that I could imagine anyone having the nerve to pinch that formidable rear.)

Ms. Robins ruled by fear, not love. Her mission was to keep the Menorah Residence profitable and keep the residents happy, and to my mind, there was no doubt which took precedence. If people started leaving because of Schultz, that animal was toast.

Bernice rushed to tattle. "Riva's dog tried to jump on Sam's body. And he almost made me fall down. You know how dangerous that is? I could have broken a bone," she whined.

"I'll deal with it," she said. "Please go to your suites. There's no need to congregate here."

The fun seemed to be over, and people wandered off, whispering to one another. But I stayed on.

"Ms. Robins," I called, as she retreated to her office. "Can I speak to you?"

"Yes, come in, Ellie. I want to talk to you too. Please sit down."

Her office was as tidy and impersonal as she was, with nothing on view but a desk, filing cabinets and a few chairs. There were no family photos or other knick-knacks in this austere place. The desk was strategically placed in the corner opposite the door, which gave Ms. Robins a full view of the goings on in the lobby and entrance. Not much escaped her. Did she have a life outside the Menorah? If she did, no one knew about it.

I took a deep breath.

"It's about Riva's dog. I know that some people here think she should get rid of it."

"They certainly do, and I'm not sure that I don't agree with them. That animal is noisy and uncontrolled and dangerous. We're considering changing the rules about residents owning animals," she said. "If someone trips over the dog and gets hurt, we could get sued. Surely you realize that."

She spoke slowly and loudly as if she were talking to someone with sub-par intellect. Did she think I was deaf? She shuffled papers on her desk, so I could see how little time she had for the kind of nonsense I was talking.

"I understand," I said, "but there are other considerations here. Did you know that Riva is a Holocaust survivor? Her parents sent her to England from Nazi Germany when she was a child, with the Kindertransport rescue operation, so that she could escape, even though they couldn't. Neither of her parents survived, and she lived with her adoptive parents until she married and came to the United States. She's a widow with a daughter who lives far away. The dog means a lot to her."

That caught Ms. Robins' attention. She dropped the papers, looking a trifle dismayed. "No, I didn't know that. She certainly keeps it quiet."

"She doesn't talk about her background, but if word gets out that she left the Menorah Residence because you didn't allow her to keep her dog, the one living being she loves in the world except for her daughter, it wouldn't look good. People wouldn't want to come live here.

"I can see the headlines now," I said craftily. (Oh, it was delicious baiting Ms Bossypants!) "'Octogenarian Holocaust survivor kicked out into the streets by the Menorah Residence.' Or maybe, 'My dog and I: all alone in the world, thanks to the cruel Menorah management team.'"

This was fun. I was getting into my stride. "How about..."

Ms. Robins hastily stopped me. "Ok, thank you, Ellie. That's enough."

She drummed her French-polished manicured nails on the desk and pondered.

"How do you know? Did she tell you?"

That was the part I didn't want to go into. Naturally, Riva hadn't told me. She didn't tell me anything. I had discovered her background in the course of my browsing in the Community Archive. It was just my natural nosiness at work, I guess.

By chance, I had been leafing through a book about the Kindertransport, which I had learned was an organized rescue effort that took place before the outbreak of the Second World War and which brought children to the United Kingdom to save them from the Nazis. Hal, the new guy in the Archive, had seen me reading it, and had mentioned that one of the residents of the Menorah, Riva Manheim, had actually been a Kindertransport child herself. I asked him how he had learned that, and he had replied that Riva often came to the Archive and they had become friends.

Fascinated, I took the book away to read. I knew that Kindertransport means "Children's transport" in German, but what

I hadn't known was that nearly 10,000 children from Germany, Austria, Czechoslovakia and Poland had been sent to foster homes far away to escape from the World War. Some were still babies.

How terrible it must have been for parents to send their children away, knowing that they might never see them again. And how terrible for the children to be taken away from their parents, to a strange country where they knew no one and didn't speak the language. Still, they were the lucky ones. They survived. What Riva must have suffered! I was willing to forgive all her snobbery, knowing her story.

Ms Robins was waiting to hear my answer. I told her the truth.

"No, she didn't tell me. I found out from the man who works in the Community Archive."

She looked thoughtful. I figured it was time to change the subject and bring up my killer argument for saving Schultz: "I can help look after the dog. I'll make sure it doesn't cause any more problems."

"Hmm. I'll give it some thought, and in the meantime, I'll have a talk with Riva. But there's another matter. I understand you made the, what do you call them, those stuffed dumplings that were served for lunch?"

"The knishes? Yes, I did."

She leaned forward and looked me in the eye.

"Sam collapsed after eating one of them. Are you sure you didn't make a mistake in the recipe, and maybe added something that shouldn't be there? By mistake, of course. You know, when we get older, dear, we tend to become absentminded."

What, she was intimating that I poisoned Sam? By mistake, of course. Also that I was losing it. And the 'dear'? That was patronizing. In fact, it was outrageous.

I bristled. "No, I didn't make a mistake!"

"Calm down, Ellie," she said gently, "I don't know why you potter around in the kitchen at all. Our staff doesn't need help. Why don't you just make cookies in your microwave? Not that those of us of ample build," she added, eying my waistline, "need extra cookies. Now run along. I'll think about what you told me."

I was dismissed. Ample build! I wasn't going to forget that insult. Darned if that skinny sanctimonious bat was going to keep me out of the kitchen.

❧ Chapter Four ❦

Normally, my pleasant, disorderly small apartment, with its mid-century vintage Scandinavian-style furniture (now surprisingly back in fashion) and scattering of books and magazines, soothed me, but today I couldn't settle down. Of course a sudden death was shocking, but heck, it happened often enough around here. At our age, it wasn't unexpected. I hadn't even liked Sam that much. What had really thrown me was that he had dropped dead so suddenly in a way you wouldn't wish on anybody. When I went, I hoped it wouldn't be with knish crumbs on my face. (Although come to think of it, with my appetite, it wouldn't be all that unlikely.)

Two hours after his death, I still felt shaken by Sam's death, which wasn't good for me. Stress, I knew, was a trigger for an asthma attack, and sure enough, my chest felt tight and I was beginning to wheeze. I reached for my trusty inhaler, which I always kept nearby.

The inhaler helped, but I needed something more to calm me down. Baking... that's what I needed to do. Of course! What could be more comforting than the fresh tang of lemon peel, the delicious aroma of vanilla, the satisfying thwack of yeasty dough pummeled into shape? Baking made me feel, if not exactly young again, at least useful.

Some people took Valium when they were stressed; some lost

21

themselves in the TV soaps, but for me, food—preparing it, enjoying it—was what relaxed me most. When I died, I wanted to go to Williams-Sonoma heaven. Meanwhile, I kneaded dough for fun.

I decided that I would give myself a challenge and prepare apple strudel, an old family favorite, and take it to the kitchen to be baked. If Ms. Robins didn't like it, well, nuts to her. I would stay out of her way.

I wrapped my apron around my waist, reached into my tiny fridge for the butter and dove in.

Unlike many bakers, I never used ready-made pastry for strudel. I remember my grandmother making *lokshen*—the Yiddish term for noodles—by stretching dough paper thin until it enveloped the whole dining room table, which had been covered with a freshly-laundered tablecloth, and then rolling up the dough and slicing it into strips. In those days, we scorned her home-made efforts and longed for packaged noodles like everyone else had. Today, we would call her *lokshen* "pasta" and hail her as a foodie.

So that was the method I used. With the dough prepared, I spread my small vintage chrome and Formica kitchen table with a fresh cloth and floured it all liberally. Then I stretched the dough paper-thin over the cloth and sat down to let the dough rest.

My thoughts returned to Sam. I remembered, suddenly, the pill that had fallen out of the knish. How very odd! Why would he put a pill in a knish that he planned to juggle? Surely if he needed to take medicine with the meal, he would just have swallowed it with a glass of water? And what was the pill? Could it have contributed to his heart attack?

I reached into my pocket and pulled out the crumbling half pill. It was round and yellow and had the letters "vil" on it. It didn't mean a thing to me.

A knock at the door startled me. I was astonished to see Riva, who had never visited me before, with, of course, her dog Schultz.

"Excuse me," she said formally." I don't wish to bother you, but I wondered how you were," she said. "I know that you have asthma and I hoped that you didn't have an attack. Also, I saw you rub your back after you caught my Schultz. Did you hurt yourself?"

I was quite heartened. This was good to hear; it seemed she

wasn't angry about the part I had played in the dog fiasco. On the contrary, I had earned her approval.

"I'm fine. Just embarrassed at the spectacle I made of myself," I said as I waved her in.

Riva had a slight European accent and definitely stood out as an odd bird among this flock of mid-Western hens. A tiny woman who used the aid of a walker, she was always neatly turned out in well-cut skirts and polished orthopedic shoes, outfits that couldn't be more unlike the pants, wash and wear blouses and sports shoes that most of the rest of us wore. She was one of the few women here who didn't color her hair and made no attempt to look younger than she was. The fact that she also kept very much to herself made her seem even more of an oddity at the Menorah Residence.

Now, though, she was showing another side of herself.

"I also heard that you spoke to Ms. Robins about Schultz. She just called me in and told me that you offered to help look after him. I admit that sometimes he is too much for me. I would appreciate the help."

"No problem! I love dogs."

Actually, no one but Riva could love that mutt, but I was willing to pitch in. And also, I had to admit it was fun to see everyone run for cover when he appeared. Schultz was now hanging around the fridge expectantly. I reached inside and retrieved a cookie, which I threw to him.

Riva looked around. I wonder what she made of my minimalist décor, which was entirely lacking the quilts and doilies that most residents went for. Then she spied my dough stretched out on the table and her eyes lit up. "You are making apfel strudel! I used to help my mother prepare that."

Then you must help me too," I said, making room at the small table. "Shall we peel and chop the apples? Or did your mother grate them?"

"Ah, but you must take away your medication first," Riva said, pointing to Sam's pill, which I had absent-mindedly left on the counter next to the chopping board. "You wouldn't want to bake it into the apfel strudel!"

Riva actually had a sense of humor, sort of! Who knew?

Should I tell her? I decided that I would.

"No, that isn't my medication. Actually, it's part of a pill that fell out of the knish Sam was eating. I picked it up from the floor."

"And you are thinking that maybe it caused Sam's death?" She had leapt to the same conclusion I had.

"Yes, that's exactly what I did think. But it's ridiculous. He wouldn't have stuck the pill in the knish himself, so it would have to mean that someone else would have done it—someone who wanted him to feel ill, or even die. Why would any of the *alte kakers* here have wanted to harm Sam? He was just a silly old ham."

"But maybe he wasn't," Riva said warmly. "Maybe someone did want to hurt him. Ordinary people can easily do that."

Of course she would think that, given her history. I caught her excitement. "Do you think we should tell Ms. Robins about the pill?"

"No. She will just think we are becoming senile. I think it is time to show her that even though we are old, we are intelligent people who are capable of drawing correct conclusions. We will find out about the pill for ourselves. We will go to his room and look at his medications. Perhaps he was taking this one. Or perhaps this pill interacts with something that he was taking. If so, it would be..." She tailed off.

I was shocked, appalled and—dare I say it—thrilled. This was the most excitement we'd had since Mrs. Maltz had accused the kitchen of cooking her cat.

"It would be murder!"

With gleeful relish, Riva, the woman I'd assumed was a thoroughly high-minded snob, said, "Yes. It would."

✌ Chapter Five ✌

We left the dough on the table. Heck, who needed apple, uh, apfel strudel when we had a possible murder on our hands!

Still, I saw a problem. "Riva, how will we get into his room? It's probably locked."

"I will manage this," she said, heading for the hall remarkably quickly with the aid of her walker. I hastily followed her. Sam's suite was on my floor, about ten doors away. The door was indeed locked, but one of the cleaners was wheeling her cart down the hall. I knew her, of course. It was Katerine, a gentle woman who came from Cuba and often worked double shifts. We knew that she sent much of the money she earned home to her family.

"Katerine, my dear, it is good to see you," Riva said, her accent suspiciously stronger than usual. And was that a limp she was putting on?

"How is your darling daughter?"

"She's fine, Mrs. Mannheim. Thank you for asking. And how are you? You seem to be having trouble walking today."

"Ach, I am getting old. The pain... there is little I can do for it. And I am using my old walker that doesn't help me very much. Sam borrowed my other walker and he has not returned it yet. But since he died, poor man, I have no way of getting it back."

She sighed heavily.

I was impressed. What a performance!

25

"Don't you worry, you poor thing," said Katerine warmly. "I'll let you in and you can look for the walker. I'll lock up when I finish here. Just don't tell anyone. We aren't supposed to do this."

"You are so good to me, Katerine, I certainly won't tell anyone," Riva said as she hobbled into the opened room. You bet she won't, I thought, as I followed.

"Er... I'll help her look for the walker."

Katerine smiled and continued pushing her cart down the hall. We were in!

"You take the bedroom and I'll take the bathroom," I suggested. The bathroom was bound to be more fun.

The suite had little personality. There were no pictures of Sam's late wife or his children; in fact no pictures at all other than a painting on velvet of a green-faced woman on one wall. I noticed a television, a rather threadbare orange and brown shag carpet and a worn recliner chair. A beige sofa was covered in plastic. What was he preserving the furniture for, I wondered. His old age?

It was surprising that someone as colorful as Sam should live in such a bland apartment, and even more surprising that so little money had been spent on it.

I started opening drawers in the bathroom. Yikes! What was that? A spider? Oh, a toupee. I knew it! No one has hair like Sam at his age. This must be a spare one.

"Riva, I found his toupee," I shouted.

"Please be quieter, Ellie. Look for the medicine, not for evidence of his secret vanities. They are of no interest to us."

They're of interest to me, I thought. Riva could be a bit of a downer sometimes.

In the well-stocked medicine cabinet, I reached for his medication dispenser, which had compartments for each of the days of the week and for morning, mid-day and evening of each day. I opened the section for today, Wednesday. The morning and mid-day sections were empty, naturally, since he had dutifully taken his pills. The Thursday sections were full. I emptied them out in my hand.

There were the blood pressure medications that I took myself and sure enough, the little yellow pill that matched the one I had picked up. It was marked "Elavil." Yup, that was it. I found the box from which the Elavil pill had been taken and pulled out the package insert, with its description of the drug and information on its usage. We could read that later and figure out if it was dangerous.

"Hurry, Ellie. Katerine will be coming back," whispered Riva urgently.

"Sure, right away," I said, without moving. I was busy checking out the rest of the medications.

Well, well. Three packets of Viagra. So Sam was being frisky with someone. Could that be a motive for killing him? I pocketed the Viagra. He wouldn't be needing it anymore, and why embarrass his family when they came to clean out his suite?

Time to go. I joined Riva in the living room.

"I found the yellow pill. Also some Viagra. What did you discover?"

"Only a few bottles of whiskey and two empty bottles in the bedroom cupboard," said Riva. "It seems that he did not want people to know that he drank." That made me smile. Where did he think he lived? Of course just everyone knew.

Sam's computer stood on a small table near the sofa, desktop pattern glowing. What luck! We wouldn't need to log in.

"We've gone this far, we might as well continue snooping, uh, inspecting for clues," I said. "After all," I added virtuously, "we're simply trying to solve a possible murder." Riva looked dubious, but made no objection.

Among the desk top icons was one for JLove. That wasn't unusual; a lot of residents were registered on the dating site, which specialized in matches for Jewish singles. There were no age limits on love and even 80 year olds lived in hope. I knew this because every evening, a clutch of eager women gathered around the computer in the library. Not everyone had a computer or could work one, so they used the library facility to check out the talent on JLove.

I couldn't resist. I clicked on the icon, which went straight to Sam's profile. *About me*, I read. *I am a 76 year old widower*.

"He's says he's 76! Didn't we celebrate his 84th birthday in the last joint birthday party?"

Riva peered over my shoulder and smiled.

"Listen to this: *I'm 6 feet tall'*... I burst out laughing. Maybe on stilts he was. *People say I'm funny and very sexy. I still have all my hair.*

"Right. He still has all his hair in his bathroom drawer," I said. I continued reading.

I'm a retired entrepreneur, looking for an established woman with elegance and humor.

By this time, both of us were laughing.

"I believe he ran a small hardware shop, did he not?" asked Riva.

"Yes, he did. I suppose that's entrepreneurship. But the really important thing here is that he's looking for an 'established' woman. That's code for 'rich'. He's out for money."

I clicked on the list of women who had sent emails or 'flirted' with him online.

"Wow! There must be 20 women here. No wonder he kept a supply of Viagra."

And there was a picture of Joyce! It had been taken in her salad days, but was still recognizably her even though she called herself "Magda." Well, well. If Joyce had replied—and I still couldn't believe what I was seeing—no doubt there were other women from the Menorah on his string of devotees as well. Good grief. Sam was a Lothario; a one-man dating service.

"Ellie," Riva pulled my sleeve. "We really must leave."

"Just a minute." I pulled out the drawer under the computer to see what other delicious goodies I could discover. And bingo! A pile of $100 bills. Definitely, this was suspicious. His son was unlikely to have given him cash, since he lived hundreds of miles away. If he was helping Sam out, he would transfer money through the bank or send a check for his personal expenses, and pay for the Menorah fees directly. It wasn't very likely that he would be sending Sam that much money anyway. That meant that the pile of hundred dollar bills had to come from somewhere else. But where? Could it be that Sam was extorting money?

True, there might be a legitimate reason he had a stash of cash, but I really couldn't think of one. And if the money came from a less than legitimate source, there was one conclusion we could draw: Sam, it appeared, was not just a harmless joker after all. And someone might have a motive to do him in.

I turned back to the computer. We had to find out more. Riva put her hand over mine, as I hovered over the keyboard about to press the "Finances" icon. "No," she said. "That is not our business."

"Sorry. You're right," I said, lying in my teeth and casting a reluctant glance at the tempting icon.

"You don't need to be sorry. Your curiosity and love of life are qualities that I like about you."

I was inordinately pleased, like a shy high school student who had just been complimented by the football team's star quarterback.

"They are? I didn't know you liked anything about anyone here."

Of course I was fishing for a compliment, and I caught one.

"I know that people here think that I am a snob, and perhaps I am, but my life has been so different that I feel I have very little in common with people here. But you... you have optimism and a sense of humor that I respect."

I turned red. I would savor this compliment later, but right now we had things to do. I looked at the package insert and skimmed the page. Elavil, it appeared, was a trycyclic antidepressant called amitrypyline, taken for depression. I couldn't think of anyone who seemed less depressed than Sam, but clearly you never knew.

"Now here's something," I said. "There can be side effects if taken with alcohol. A heart attack is one of the possibilities. That's obviously what happened."

Riva mused. "He could have taken the pill himself and not known about the side effects."

"No. He already took his pills this morning. This was another pill altogether. In fact, there could have been more than one pill in the knish. There could have been a half dozen. In effect, it was an overdose, and in combination with the alcohol, it could have caused his collapse. We have to figure out who knew what he was taking, knew what might happen and knew about his drinking habit."

"Everyone knew about his drinking," said Riva. "You said so yourself. But there is another thing: who had the opportunity to put the pill, or pills, into his knishes? Who knew which were the knishes meant for his table? It could only be someone in the kitchen or dining room."

We heard a clattering, as Katerine's cart lumbered down the hall towards us.

"Let's get out of here," I whispered.

"Very well. We will return to your strudel and think about this."

"The heck with the strudel," I said, grinning and heading for the door. "I'm off to the kitchen to see if I can discover how the pills got into my knishes."

❧ Chapter Six ❧

"Hi Maurice!" I breezed through the door of the modern, industrial kitchen, which was just as upmarket as the rest of the Menorah. It had gleaming stainless steel work counters, banks of ovens and cooking tops and a huge industrial freezer room at the back. The kitchen was particularly large because it was kosher, meaning that there were duplicate appliances, dishes and cutlery for meat and milk meals.

"Ellie, sweetie, I'm so glad you're here." Maurice sounded harassed and upset. "We can use your help."

"Sure. I'm happy to help. But first, can you tell me who had access to the knishes before they were served?"

Maurice looked at me oddly.

"Who had access? The entire kitchen staff, of course, plus everyone who wandered through, like Ms Robins and some of the residents who were curious about what was going to be served. It's Grand Central Station here. Why on earth do you ask?"

"No reason."

That certainly shed no light on who might have stuffed the knishes with a pill. And how did the pill get to Sam's knish, rather than anyone else's? We would have to figure that out.

Meanwhile, Tommy, the chef, was leafing through his tattered recipe book. I peered over his shoulder.

"I guess you're working on the *shiva* menu, right?"

"Yeah. Ms. Robins is on my case. She's scared that something Sam ate may have caused him to collapse and she wants us to be extra careful about what we prepare. So in addition to the kosher inspector driving me crazy, I have to worry about making food that won't make anyone sick. As if it's my fault that Sam checked out. And that's not the only problem. Sam's family is flying in right away and they aren't wasting time holding the funeral. It's tomorrow. That leaves us practically no time to get ready."

Although the *shiva* (literally, "seven"), the Jewish mourning ritual in which friends pay their respects to the mourners following the funeral, is traditionally held for seven full days, it was more common at the Menorah for it to be scheduled for only a few hours on one or two days. That was because the family was often from out of town and had to return home, or was not religiously observant. However, it was considered common courtesy for everyone who knew the deceased or the family to come to the *shiva*. Many of those who attended also participated in the afternoon or evening prayer service which was held during that time.

Not that a *shiva* was considered something to avoid, or that anyone here would dream of missing one. *Shiva* was a very big deal—on one hand because it marked the death of a friend, but on the other hand (to be perfectly honest) because of the food—not to mention the schnapps, or whiskey, that was a necessary part of the occasion.

It may have been solemn, but the *shiva* was a social occasion, often spiced with gossip about the generosity, or otherwise, of the family sponsoring the spread.

I grinned. "Remember Nathan Landberg's *shiva* last year?" Tommy and Maurice guffawed.

The family had tried to save money by having the kitchen provide only fruit plates and cookies at the *shiva*. There wasn't any liquor either. Cheapskates! People walked out. That left the rabbi without a *minyan*, or obligatory minimum of 10 participants, for prayers. Ever since then, *shiva* occasions at the Menorah had been lavishly catered by kitchen staff, for a fee, of course.

"Luckily for us," Tommy said, "price isn't a factor this time. Sam's son has been in touch with the office and said that we should just prepare whatever we think is appropriate for the *shiva*."

"Generous of him," I thought, wondering why his open handedness hadn't extended to his father while he was alive. He could have sprung for some better furniture for Sam's room. But perhaps they weren't on good terms. I would have to look into that possibility.

"What should we make?"

"Well, not knishes," I joked. That fell flat. Tommy glared at me.

I hurriedly changed the subject. "What about cheese blintzes? Everybody loves them. We could serve them with strawberries and sour cream."

Tommy looked dubious. "That's a ton of work. And we don't have a lot of time."

"So who cares? Sam's son is paying. You can charge him a lot extra because of all the labor involved. I'll help."

He perked up. "Yes, it might work. That will make the office happy. Ms. Robins has been after me a lot lately to cut costs. I think the Menorah might be in some financial trouble. They've hired a new accountant to look into things and I believe the owners are coming around on an inspection tour too."

Maurice stared, grim-faced. "An inspection tour?" He leaned on the prep table, his face suddenly pale. We looked at him quizzically. Tommy raised an eyebrow.

"What?" he snapped at our concerned looks. "Let's get on with it."

I was shocked. Why would Maurice react so badly to the news that the Menorah management was going to check into expenditures? He handled kitchen purchases and expenses; could Sam have found evidence of cheating and been blackmailing him? Could that be a motive for murder? Was Maurice a suspect? I felt dizzy. The list of possible suspects was growing by the hour!

Tommy had gone to the walk-in refrigerator, next to the huge freezer, to check on supplies. Whistling, he brought out milk, eggs and cream cheese and retrieved flour and oil from the pantry. He was interrupted by Bernice, who had wandered astray into the kitchen again and was looking around blankly. Tommy steered her to the door and she set off happily to wherever she was headed. Bernice was a walking comedy routine, but she did lighten the atmosphere.

"Maurice," I said as soon as we were alone. "We're friends. You can tell me. What's wrong?"

For the first time, I noticed that his handsome face looked worn.

"I know I can trust you, darling. The truth is, I have been, uh, making an arrangement with one of the vendors about his food bills."

"What? You've been taking kickbacks?"

He winced. "I wouldn't call it that. Just... a favor to the fruit and vegetable guy in return for a favor for me."

"A kickback, in other words."

"Ok, a kickback." He looked uncomfortable. "And Sam was onto me. He came into the kitchen one day while the produce guy was handing over some cash and figured it out right away. The next day, he intimated that he wanted me to split the proceeds with him. When Tommy mentioned just now that Ms. Robins was getting in accountants to check on expenses, I thought Sam might have told her."

"Why would he do that if he stood to gain by blackmailing you? No, I'm sure he didn't tell her. But..." I looked at him in horror.

Maurice looked at me reproachfully. He knew very well what had crossed my mind.

"Ellie," he said, shaking his head. "What kind of conclusions are you jumping to? Are you thinking that I might have been responsible for his death? That I might even have poisoned him? That's insane."

"Although," he added, lowering his voice, "There were people who disliked him. In the unlikely event that he was knocked off, I do have my suspicions about who might have done it."

"Who?"

"No." He shook his head. "I don't want to say. I might be wrong. But it wasn't me! What do you take me for?"

What did I take him for? A thief, that's what. But no, Maurice was my friend, and he couldn't be a murderer too.

Could he?

❧ Chapter Seven ❧

Social affairs being rather thin on the ground once people got to our stage of life, we make the most of the ones we have. A *shiva* wasn't what most people would call a dress-up occasion, but at the Menorah, a well-catered *shiva* rated up there with bar mitzvahs and New Year's Eve. (It was even more important than New Year's Eve, come to think about it, because none of us could stay up until midnight.)

I paid more attention to my appearance than I usually did, because to tell the truth, I thought that Hal, the guy I fancied from the Community Archive, might be there. Sam had visited the Community Archive from time to time, or so I had heard, and it would be only polite of Hal to pay his respects. I hoped so, anyway.

It's hard to be glamorous when you love food. The truth was that Ms Robins was right, darn her. I did have an ample build, if that's what you wanted to call it. That rankled. I looked in the mirror and sighed. Then I took off my glasses so that everything looked fuzzy, in the hopes that would make me look thinner. No such luck. I knew I shouldn't have eaten all those blintzes, even though it was all in the line of duty, and even though I knew I'd eat them again, given the chance. It all seemed quite hopeless. I munched on a cookie for consolation.

The outfit I chose in the end was a cowl-necked blouse in soft pink, which I wore with black silk pants. A little bit daring, a little bit classic—it seemed to fill the bill. The pants, admittedly, had elastic in the back, but no one would ever know, because the top, which wasn't tucked in, hid the technicalities. Since Louboutin doesn't make flats with room for a bunion, I added tasteful black patent Clarks shoes. Once I had hauled my bra straps in a northerly direction and tossed a paisley scarf over my shoulder, I was ready. Well, as ready as I'd ever be.

The *shiva* was held in the library, a large, wood-panelled multi-purpose room with comfortable armchairs, bookshelves and the public computer in one corner. It was on the mezzanine floor, and one side, which overlooked the entrance hall below, was open. The room was used for private parties and other events and also served as the ad hoc synagogue on Friday evenings and Saturday mornings, when a local rabbi came in to officiate at services. On those occasions, folding chairs were taken out, and a Torah scroll and a small pulpit were removed from a locked closet and set up.

The library was a popular place for residents to hang out because of its location overlooking the main entrance, which provided a good vantage point if you wanted to see who was coming and going without being seen yourself.

As usual, people gathered early to express their sympathies to the mourners. The formalities observed, they made straight for the table, which had a respectable spread, including bagels, cream cheese and lox, tea and coffee, and of course, my blintzes, accompanied by crystal dishes of sour cream and strawberry preserve. The blintzes looked pretty good, I thought, and the way people were digging in, they tasted good too. Take that, Ms. Robins!

On a side table stood bottles of whiskey, gin and vodka, with glasses, ice and mixers. That was also well patronized.

Of course the visitors had just had lunch and could hardly be hungry, but as Mollie put it, "What has hunger got to do with it?"

At the entrance to the library, the solemn family of mourners— Sam's son Milton, his wife and two teenage grandchildren—were greeting visitors.

"I'm so sorry for your loss," I said to Milton. "Sam will be missed here. He had a wonderful sense of humor."

"Thank you. Yes, he did. Have you met my wife Joy and our sons Justin and Noah?"

Justin looked about 10 years old and seemed awed into silence by the occasion. Noah, on the other hand, was a typical teen: he had an unfortunate skin condition, his sneakers were untied, his hair worn in spikes and he was paying more attention to his cell phone than to the people shuffling by. If he had cared at all for his grandfather, it certainly didn't show. I heard a few whispered comments in the background about "the kids of today," which clearly embarrassed his parents.

Joy poked him, which irritated him enough to be provoking.

"Right, a sense of humor," he said, cracking his gum. "Like the time he stole his partner's share of the profits and ended up in jail."

"Noah!" his father hissed through gritted teeth. "Behave."

"Chill, Daddio."

Joy, embarrassed, tried to extricate herself. "Kids today! They make up stories just to get attention."

It was a pretty weak way to salvage the situation, but under the circumstances, the best she could do. Then she thought better of it. Obviously, she had decided that since no one was fool enough to believe that Noah had made up the story about Sam, she had better tell me the truth and try to hush me up. While her husband continued to greet guests (and Noah checked his phone), she took me aside.

"Please don't let this get around," she said. "It's true that Sam spent a few months in prison, but it was because he had a gambling habit and he wanted money. It was a long time ago, and since then, Milt has kept control of his finances. Sam only needed to ask if he needed money, and he didn't ask for more than his usual allowance, which we kept small, so we knew he wasn't gambling any more. We were sure that he was managing well."

I nodded. "Of course."

His allowance had been kept small. Hmm. So the stash of hundred dollar bills we had found in his suite hadn't come from his son.

But I wondered how many people had heard what Joyce had told me. Mollie, who had sharp ears for her age, had been standing nearby. If she had overheard, Sam's stint as a jailbird would be common knowledge by dinner time. In fact, Mollie was already whispering in a corner to a crowd that included Pearl,

Bernice and a clutch of other residents. They looked positively thrilled at what they were hearing. The secret was clearly out.

So there was no longer any point in keeping this juicy information to myself and I couldn't wait to tell Riva the hot news. I looked around and spotted her talking to... oy... Hal.

I pulled in my stomach.

"Ellie!" Riva called me over. "I have been telling Hal about your kind offer to help look after my Schultz. He has a dog also."

"Yes, I brought Coco with me from San Diego," Hal said pleasantly. "She's been the best company ever since my wife died. It would be a real shame if the Menorah administrators decided that animals weren't allowed to stay here anymore."

Hal was about my age, but on him, it looked good. Unlike myself, the only thing ample about him was his height. Tall, rangy and white-haired with an air of easy-going amiability, he reminded me a little of Fred Rogers, the late, beloved children's television program host. I heard he even had a motorcycle—well, a motor scooter—as well as a car. A cool Mr. Rogers—was that perfection or what?

But maybe I was reading too much into this; for all I knew, he could be a total jerk. Nevertheless, I couldn't help warming to Hal. He had an engaging smile that melted my heart. He was smiling now. At me! I took deep breaths to calm my racing pulse.

"It really would be a shame if pets were banned, but I think that Schultz is in trouble after the chaos he caused today," I said. "We'll have to keep him out of sight, or at least out of Ms. Robins' sight."

"I heard about that," said Hal. "Why don't you bring him round to the Community Archive the next time you come? He can't get up to too much mischief there."

"Yes!" I thought to myself. You bet. Taking Schultz for walkies to the Community Archive would give me an excuse to get to know Hal better.

In spite of Mollie's best efforts, no one knew much about Hal, other than the fact that he was retired, lived in an apartment complex nearby, and volunteered four days a week to help out in the Community Archive, which was located next door to the Menorah Residence. Naturally, he was a great subject of gossip.

Mollie said she'd heard that he was a plastic surgeon from Los

Angeles who had been sued because he destroyed the face of a movie actress and had to leave town. She said she read it in a tabloid. (Of course that would make it true.) Sam, on the other hand, who was probably jealous, had hinted strongly that he knew Hal was up to no good. Exactly what he was doing that was no good, Sam didn't know, but no good for sure.

Some of the other rumors making the rounds were that he was a spy for the nearby Mount Carmel Retirement Residence, which was trying to steal away clients from the Menorah; that he was gay; that he was married and had left his wife; and that he was a porn star. That last rumor was pretty far out, even by the standards of our resident crew, but Jake Diamond said he'd seen him in a porn film on television. (Of course, that led to further scandal about the fact that Jake had admitted to watching porn. His wife was currently not speaking to him as a result.)

I thought the gossip was nonsense, but still, it all seemed a little mysterious. Aurora was a pleasant enough town, but choosing to live in Minnesota and freeze in the winter, when you could live anywhere? Nobody could figure it out. Hal himself was polite, but no help. He just wasn't very forthcoming.

"What's everyone so excited about," he asked now, looking around. "Something must be up because nobody is at the food."

"Well, it appears that Sam spent some time in jail. He cheated his partner, because he needed money to gamble. But his daughter-in-law told me that they controlled his money, and he no longer gambled."

"Really? But he had money in his room. So where did he get it? Was he blackmailing someone? A girlfriend?" Riva asked, jumping to conclusions. "That would be a good reason to kill him."

Hal was curious. "You think he was killed? But he had a heart attack."

"Yes," I said. "But his heart attack could have been caused by a fatal drug interaction with alcohol. We found evidence in his room."

"You cased his room, like amateur detectives?" Hal had a nice laugh—deep and contagious. "You two have hidden depths."

"Yup. Just call us Miss Marplestein and Shoirlok Hertz," I said in an exaggeratedly nasal Brooklyn accent.

We were interrupted by Ms. Robins, who was striding around

looking annoyed. Since that was her default expression though, no one was paying much attention.

"Where is Maurice? The table is a mess and we're out of coffee here. The Levins are complaining."

"I saw him a few minutes ago in the kitchen," I told her.

"Well he isn't there now. Could you please go look again, Ellie? You know the kitchen well enough." That was a sly dig at my ignoring her instructions to stay out of the kitchen. Never mind that my blintzes had saved her money.

She frowned. "Oh, and while you're there, could you bring back another pot of coffee?

Her peremptory orders, as if I were a staff member, infuriated me, but I nodded. At least I could tip off Maurice that Ms. Robins was on the warpath. The sight of the laden table stopped me momentarily, and I grabbed a bagel. Why not? I hadn't eaten. Well, not very much. Why take a chance on everything good disappearing before I got back? And that lox looked tempting.

"Ellie." Ms Robins gritted her teeth. "Please. Now."

Gripping my bagel, annoyingly without lox, I took the stairs down from the mezzanine to the ground floor and headed for the kitchen, meeting Bernice on the way. She had obviously been to the bathroom, since she was trailing a piece of toilet paper. What was with this woman and the bathroom? I removed the paper, and pointed out the way to the library.

Odd. Maurice wasn't there and neither was Tommy or anyone from the kitchen staff, come to think of it. I looked in the pantry. No one there either. Oh well. They were probably smoking a forbidden cigarette outside.

The only one in the kitchen was Schultz, whimpering next to the freezer at the back of the room.

"What are you doing here?" I asked the silly mutt. "You aren't allowed in the kitchen. Riva's probably looking for you. If Ms. Robins sees you here, you can count on a one-way trip to the pound. Schultz, you are in such trouble."

He whimpered, running back and forth between me and the door of the walk-in freezer.

"You're not going to find any food worth eating in there," I said. "Go home!

Now he was jumping up on his hind legs with his front paws

on the door of the freezer.

"It's cold in there. Cold! Do you want to see?"

I yanked at the door of the giant, walk-in freezer, which seemed stuck for some reason. Giving it all I had, I gave one more pull at the door handle, which suddenly swung open, sending me flying backward. I landed on my bottom on top of Schultz, who squealed in protest.

Schultz crawled out from under me and jumped into my lap. The two of us stared as Maurice, blue in the face, toppled slowly out of the freezer, landing on both Schultz and me. His eyes, wide open, stared lifelessly in his bloodless face.

He was literally out cold. Dead cold. And he was in my lap!

Horrified, I could feel an asthma attack coming on, and I didn't have my inhaler with me. Would I be the next one to go?

❧ Chapter Eight ❧

"Well, that certainly ended the *shiva* with a bang," said Pearl, who had come to visit me in my suite, along with Bernice, ostensibly to find out how I was doing after the shock of having a frozen Maurice land on me, but actually to hear all the gory details and to fill me in on what I had missed.

She and Bernice had made themselves comfortable on my vintage Danish Modern teak-armed sofa with turquoise upholstery, circa 1955, which I pretended I had bought at an antique sale, but actually came from the Salvation Army. At $25, it had been a great buy, since Aurora residents hadn't yet cottoned on to the fact that mid-century furniture was now considered desirable.

Although Pearl often belittled my baking, she had had no qualms about raiding my small refrigerator for whatever seemed to be going, and helping herself to the remains of the apple strudel.

I was in bed, resting under my white duvet with a cup of sweet tea on a tray. The asthma attack had left me weak, and I still didn't feel quite like myself, although hours had passed and it was already evening. There was nothing like a corpse landing in your lap to shock the system. Poor Maurice. There would be a lot of unhappy women in the Menorah right now.

"You missed a ton of excitement," said Pearl, with relish. "When we heard you screaming and the dog yapping, everyone who could run headed for the kitchen. There was a stampede for the elevator, and so many people crowded into it that it stalled on the way down to the ground floor. Ms. Robins didn't know what to do first."

She polished off the apple strudel and helped herself to a chocolate chip cookie.

I had to laugh. Too bad I missed that.

"Then she discovered you and Maurice lying on the floor in the kitchen. Maurice was obviously stone dead. I think she thought you killed him. She shrieked and ran to her office to call the police. You were wheezing and turning red, the dog was barking and everyone in the elevator was carrying on. What an uproar! Riva brought your inhaler from your bag in the library and that revived you, but then, in the middle of everything, Joyce Kramer, that hypochondriac, was convinced she was having a heart attack and someone had to call the paramedics."

"I had to go to the bathroom," ventured Bernice.

"Sure you did," I said.

Then I thought of something.

"Did you use the restroom on this floor, or the one in your suite?"

Bernice looked puzzled. "The one on this floor. It's closer."

"And did you see anybody wandering around when you went to the restroom?"

"No. Why?"

I let it go. You got nowhere quizzing Bernice; the police could have that pleasure. And that reminded me.

"Are the police here?"

"They certainly are," said Pearl. "They're interviewing everyone under the age of 90. They were letting you rest, but I'm sure they plan to see you soon."

"I don't know what's happened to this place," she said with a sour look. "It used to be the best retirement home in town, but now look. People are dropping dead right, left and center! Mollie says that Sam was probably poisoned. She's phoned her daughter and told her that with a killer on the loose, she wants to move to her house. She was upset because her daughter didn't agree to take her immediately. And I overheard Ms Robins talking to the owners, trying to explain what had happened. It was obvious that the owners weren't buying her story. You could hear them shouting over the telephone.

"People are going to leave if this keeps up. I might myself. It might reflect badly on my granddaughter and she's engaged to a religious Jewish lawyer." She fingered her rings, unconsciously stroking her huge diamond as if to understate her granddaughter's engagement.

"Yes, we know," I said. "You've told us often enough, and I don't see how a murder here can affect their marriage."

Pearl sniffed and got up to leave. She never liked being argued with. Bernice straggled after her, casting, I swear, a backward glance at my bathroom.

Five minutes later, I heard another knock on the door. What if it were the police? Not that I had anything to do with Maurice's death, but still... I was the one who found him. What if they arrested me?

I told myself not to be ridiculous. "Come in."

Riva peeked around the door. "May we come in?" She was with Schultz, which I expected, and Hal, which I certainly did not. "How are you feeling?"

Oh God, I looked a mess. My beautiful pink blouse had coffee stains down the front and the scarf had disappeared somewhere. Dog hairs made my black silk trousers look tweedy.

"Thanks for bringing me my inhaler, Riva," I said. "It may have saved my life. I'm fine now. Just a little tired."

"I'm glad you're better," said Hal. "We were worried. Shoirlock, you have no idea what chaos your discovery has caused." He chuckled wickedly.

He was such a hunk.

I cast around for something to say. When in doubt, try food.

"Have some strudel," I suggested. He opened the fridge door and peered inside. "There's no strudel here."

"I guess Pearl finished it," I said, sighing. "Try the cookie jar."

Hal retrieved a brownie and said, "It may not be a murder after all. It could be that Maurice went into the walk-in freezer to fetch something, and then the door closed. That might make it an accident."

Riva snorted. "Of course it isn't an accident. Someone asked him to get something out of the freezer and then closed the door.

The police are idiots."

"Well," remonstrated Hal, "they haven't ruled out murder. In fact, they're interviewing everyone who might conceivably be a suspect."

"Who might that be?" I was interested in who the police thought could be a possible murderer.

"All the residents and staff," Riva said. "except those who are mentally confused, and those over the age of 90."

"Big mistake," I said. "That leaves out Mollie, who is bound to be offended. If anyone knows something, it would be Mollie. She sees everything from her sofa in the lobby."

Riva shook her head. "Three women have said they want to leave the Menorah and I am sure there will be more. Ms. Robins is in a fury. I think what makes her most angry is that the police have taken over her office to interview people."

She raised an eyebrow. "This strengthens my belief that Sam was murdered. The same person who killed him probably killed Maurice because Maurice may have suspected something. Didn't you say that he hinted something of the sort?"

I cast my mind back. "Yes, I think you're right. Maurice did tell me that he had his suspicions about Sam's death, but he didn't tell me who he suspected. That was when I was in the kitchen helping him plan the *shiva* menu. And I can tell you now something else that Maurice said to me. He admitted that he had been taking kickbacks from the produce vendor and he was afraid that with the new accountant checking all the bills and the owners planning an inspection tour, he would be found out. Could that have something to do with his death?"

"So let's think about this," Hal said. I was pleased that Hal was including himself in our amateur detection team. He could be Watson. Vatson, we would call him. I would practice my Brooklyn accent.

"Someone killed Sam. Sam had a stash of cash. Maybe he still gambled and his family didn't know and that was why he needed money. Where did it come from? Was he taking money from one of his girlfriends? Was he blackmailing somebody? Or perhaps he dumped some jealous woman."

Riva and I nodded. Those were definite possibilities.

"Pearl did say that Sam was having an affair with someone. It could be just idle gossip, or it could be a jealous lover, ridiculous as that sounds. We did find Viagra, so Pearl may be right, for a change. I'll ask her."

"As for Maurice, maybe he knew who had killed Sam and the murderer was trying to stop him from letting the cat out of the bag."

"And maybe our imaginations are running away with us," Hal cautioned. "These are pretty wild suppositions. More likely, Sam had a simple heart attack and the pill had nothing to do with it and Maurice locked himself in the freezer by mistake. Maybe the dog closed the door when he was inside."

We pondered. "Schultz did it? Nah. He's smart, but not that smart."

Riva looked displeased. She didn't like her dog disparaged, even for something as unlikely as this.

Schultz heard his name, cocked his head to one side and wagged his tail enthusiastically. A less likely murderer, even by accident, it would be hard to imagine.

"My dog would not have done such a thing. It was murder!" said Riva. She was definite.

"Meanwhile," I pointed out, "the only one who saw Maurice in the kitchen was this guy here." I pointed to Schultz, who was now ecstatically having his belly scratched by Hal. "What a pity that the only sentient being who saw the murder was a dog. I'm sure he could tell us who did it."

Schultz heard his name and barked. Clearly, he agreed.

"Who was it, boy?" asked Hal.

But answer came there none...

❧ Chapter Nine ❦

I waited for the police to contact me, the prime witness, and sure
enough, the telephone rang. It wasn't the police though. It was
my son Josh, calling from New York. Hal and Riva tactfully
pretended not to hear our conversation, although obviously there
was no way they couldn't hear my side.

"What the hell is going on there?" Josh asked. He sounded
more annoyed than worried, which come to think of it, was
probably a good thing. Being worried might lead to him doing
something I didn't like, such as interfering.

"Your administrator, Ms. Robins, called me because I'm your
next of kin. She told me that that you had an asthma attack. Then,
when I questioned her further, she admitted that some guy in the
kitchen had been locked in a freezer and had suffocated or turned
into an ice cube or something, and you were the one who found
him. Are you ok?"

"Sure, sweetie. I'm fine. It's nothing. You don't need to worry.
It was all an accident."

I didn't want to play the Jewish mother and make him feel
guilty. (I would save that for another occasion.) Also, the less he
knew about what was going on here, the better. He was even
bossier than Ms Robins.

"Well, it doesn't sound like it. I think I'll fly down one of these
days and pay you a visit. If that place can't take good care of you,

I'll move you somewhere else."

Yipes. That was all I needed. If Josh heard about the murders and our detective team, I'd be out of the Menorah quicker than you could say Jack Daniels. Or Jack Russell. Or something. And oddly enough, I didn't want to move from the Menorah now. To my surprise, I was enjoying life, which had grown a lot more exciting lately.

"Sweetheart, you don't need to come. I know how busy you are. January is a terrible month to visit Minnesota. Maybe in the summer."

But he had hung up.

While I was still pondering the possible repercussions of a visit from sharp-eyed Josh, the phone rang again. This time, it was the police. I was invited to come down to Ms. Robins' office because the police wanted to speak to me. Hmm...

"It's the police," I told Hal and Riva. "They want to talk to me. But aren't they supposed to say that it's 'just routine' and that I was needed 'to help the police with their enquiries? They should follow the script."

"Maybe the police don't read the same detective novels you do," said Hal, teasing me.

"Good luck," said Riva.

"Watch it, Shoirlock. Don't implicate us."

I gave Hal a dirty look, but he merely smiled. Hal was enjoying this. In fact, he wasn't taking this with the seriousness it deserved, in my opinion. He just seemed amused by the whole business. Wait until it was his turn to be interrogated.

In Ms. Robins' office, two police officers, a man and a woman, greeted me politely. They looked discouragingly young—in fact, about half a century younger than I was. I wondered which one was the bad cop who would try to scare me into confessing, and which was the good cop who would pretend to be on my side, so that I would confess. Hey, I'm not a fool; I watch television.

Neither of them looked as if they were about to take out the handcuffs and drag me away to a night in the cells. Too bad—that would undoubtedly raise my status around the Menorah, and also show Hal. Lieutenant Bill Johnson, as he introduced himself, was polite but bored, with a bald pate and a substantial belly. I was pleased to notice that he was polishing off a blintz, which he must have swiped from the kitchen. Aren't cops supposed to be honest? Maybe he was bent. (See? I know the jargon.)

Detective Jody Smyth, I estimated, was in her mid-30s, with an arm full of tattoos. She looked a lot tougher than her boss. With not much interest in me, she was busy looking at her cell phone.

Lieutenant Johnson finished the blintz and burped.

"Mrs. Shapiro, I believe you were the one who found the body."

"Yes, I admit it," I said.

"Admit it? Admit what?"

"I didn't kill him! I'm only admitting that I found his body! And I made those blintzes."

They smirked at each other. Detective Smyth took a deep breath. I saw myself through her eyes: an ample (read "plump") old lady who was so not with-it that she could barely walk around the block without getting confused. It was obvious she thought I was a more than usually dotty old bat. I would show her.

"I'm not accusing you of killing Mr. Levin," Lieutenant Johnson said patiently. "Just tell us please why you were in the kitchen and what exactly you saw."

"I went to the kitchen because Ms. Robins asked me to get some more coffee for the *shiva*. None of the kitchen staff were there, and when I opened the freezer door because the dog was scratching at it, Maurice toppled out. He fell on top of me. Then I screamed and everyone came running."

"And you're sure you saw nobody?"

"Well, just Schultz. He was there."

"Really?" Detective Smyth put down her cell phone and looked at me for the first time with some interest. "Who is Mr. Schultz."

"Mrs. Mannheim's dog."

They exchanged glances again.

"Thank you, Mrs. Shapiro That will be all for now. If we need to speak to you later, we'll be in touch."

Now that was ominous. I know my "Law and Order" reruns. When the detectives suspect someone of murder, they always say that they'll be in touch. In a panic, I blurted, "Maurice was my friend. I wouldn't have killed him, but he had enemies. You should look for them. Like, he had suspicions about who killed Sam."

Uh oh. Fortunately, they weren't taking me seriously. In fact Lieutenant Johnson was eyeing my cookie jar, instead of paying attention. Young people seldom do take the elderly seriously, I've found.

"Sam is the fellow who died of a heart attack and whose *shiva* was being held?" He reached into the cookie jar and retrieved a brownie, which he inspected and then bit into. I don't mind people eating my brownies, but at least wait to be asked. Don't just take them. That proves it—he was bent.

"That's right," I said. "That was Sam. And have another brownie," I added, dripping with sarcasm. It was wasted on him. He helped himself to yet another one. That was his third. I thought about mentioning his weight, and then thought again. He might mention my weight. I would take the high road and let it pass.

"He wasn't killed, Mrs. Shapiro," said Detective Smyth. It was clear she thought I was delusional, if not altogether gaga. On the other hand, it got me off the hook.

"I won't leave the city!' I shouted after them. They looked at me. "You're supposed to ask me not to leave. You forgot. What kind of cops are you?"

Detective Smyth sighed heavily. "You should lay off the reruns. But ok. Don't leave the city. And we might want to speak to you again. Happy now?"

I nodded.

That was more like it.

ॐ ॐ

"So what do we do next?"

The three of us, Riva, Hal and I, were sitting in my living room again, eating the remains of the brownies and drinking wine companionably. Schultz was gnawing on a bone left over from lunch. But to tell the truth, I was having a hard time concentrating on anything but Hal.

A lot of people believe that old folks are past it; that strong emotions like hope, affection, joy—and yes, love—are felt only by the young. But let me tell you, age makes no difference. Especially when a nice-looking man who makes your heart beat faster is sitting next to you.

What was I thinking? I never had a mid-life crisis, so maybe this was a late-life crisis?

It was funny; most of the time, I didn't really feel old. Sometimes I got a shock when I looked in the mirror and saw an elderly woman staring back. That was me? The way I felt didn't match the way I looked. In my mind, I hadn't really changed; inside, I was still the same person I had been for most of my life—pleasant-looking but nothing special, optimistic, impulsive, a little insecure. Outside., well, it was hard to get past the wrinkles.

I had never even looked at a man since Manny had died and come to think of it, before he had died either, and that was why it was so strange that I was attracted to Hal. There was a warmth and a humor about him, though, that I'd never found in anybody else, and that I really responded to.

Of course, I mused, crashing down to earth, it was ridiculous, at my age, to act like a lovesick teenager. How could I possibly imagine that this lovely man could ever like me? He had his choice of anyone, including women a lot younger than me. I had to stop thinking about him this way for my own sanity.

Hal had been pondering and he now came up with a typically sensible suggestion: "Let's start with Sam. I think the next step should be the casino. Was he really gambling?"

"Yes, he was," I said. "I know he used to go to the casino in the Menorah minibus because Mollie goes too, and she told me that he's one of the regulars. We should check on exactly how much he was losing there. Then we can follow up the love angle. Was he really having an affair with anyone here? If so, who? And could someone be jealous?"

"Yes," said Riva. "The next organized trip to the casino is on Friday. That is when we will go."

Friday was still two days ahead, but there was something I wanted to do before that. On Thursday morning, I knocked on Riva's door. A wild yapping told me that Schultz, at least, was up and ready for adventure.

"Hiya, boy," I said, when Riva let me in. Schultz stood up unsteadily on his hind legs and lurched backwards in excitement. No fool he, the terrier knew that there was likely to be something for him in this unexpected visit. And he was right. He snapped up a recently-baked cookie I had brought, drooled happily and licked my hand.

"You are friends now," said Riva. Clearly, the way to her heart was through her dog. And that was fine with me. I was happy to be Schultz's pal, if it meant I could be Riva's pal too. I liked her asperity; her no-nonsense approach to life; her lack of sentimentality. She was interesting, which was more than you could say about a lot of octogenarians.

I dropped some cookies on her table. "I thought I'd take Schultz for a walk. It's such a nice day."

That was a bit of a whopper. It was actually 15 degrees below. I kicked myself mentally for giving such a ridiculous excuse. But Riva let it go.

"Thank you, Ellie. It is most kind of you. I hope he won't be too much trouble. You will take him to the park?"

"Well, not this time." I avoided her eye. "I thought I might stop by the Community Archive. I want to check up on why Sam used to spend time there. He wasn't exactly a historian and I may find a motive for his murder, if I can discover what he was researching."

Well, it was partly true anyway.

Riva smiled knowingly. "He likes you. I can tell."

"Who, Schultz?" I asked disingenuously. Then I dropped the act. Who was I fooling? Riva wasn't the type to put up with bullshit.

"Riva, I'm over 70 and I was never a man-killer, even in my prime. I'm not beautiful or sexy. I wear big girl panties. Why would a guy like Hal be attracted to me? Because of my home-made kugel?"

"He would be attracted to you for the same reason that you are attracted to him. Because he is probably lonely and looking for companionship. Because he finds you attractive... yes, attractive... and interesting, with an open mind and a cheerful, optimistic soul. And maybe he likes kugel too! So let me hear no more of your nonsensical, teenage angst. You are ridiculous."

Yes, ma'am.

With a light heart, I clipped on Schultz's lead and headed to the entrance.

"Where are you going, Ellie?" I heard Mollie quaver from her station at the sofa in the entrance lounge. From the corner of my eye, I caught Ms. Robins, seated at her desk with the door to her office open, looking at me quizzically too.

I ignored them both. The heck with those two nosy biddies. They couldn't spoil my good mood. Nobody could.

I would have to do this before Josh arrived.

"Because he finds you attractive."

I grinned and with a bounce in my step, left.

❧ Chapter Ten ❧

A snowstorm was brewing, and the temperature had sunk to 15 degrees below. That wasn't unusual in Minnesota and I was used to it, but it didn't mean I liked it. There were times when I thought my son and daughter, who lived in pleasanter climes, had the right idea. Then again, I love the other seasons here, and in particular, the friendliness and helpfulness of people who live in the mid-West. I bet staff members, Ms Robins aside, weren't as pleasant and caring in retirement homes in California as they were here.

I put on my lined boots and my parka, wound a woolly scarf around my neck and set out. Fortunately, I didn't have far to go. The Menorah Residence was right next door to the Melvin and Sarah Witberg Jewish Heritage Community Archive. This wasn't coincidence; both had been built by the same benefactor on the adjoining plots of land.

Our town, Aurora, was lucky enough to have had a far-sighted and wealthy donor who had believed that in order to document the city's Jewish history, there should be a Jewish Community Archive, as well as a retirement home. And so he built them both—as well as sundry other general institutions such as hospital wards and university departments.

Witberg, alas, had since moved on to Minneapolis, but the institutions he had sponsored remained. The locals were proud of the Community Archive and it was frequently used by adults who were interested in local history and by schoolchildren, who were preparing school projects on their family's roots.

"Morning, Hal, I said, as Schultz and I walked into the cluttered Community Archive. It consisted of several rooms: an office and reading area, with two desks, computer stations and comfortable chairs, and a file room, which had floor to ceiling metal shelves crammed with newspaper binders, dusty folders, papers and books. Historical photographs of long-forgotten social occasions hung on the wall. It was cozy and welcoming. But what had Sam been looking for here? Could it have some bearing on why he was killed?

"Hi, there," said Hal agreeably. "Welcome to the Community Archive. I see you've brought along Schultz. He's interested in his family roots too?"

"Undoubtedly," I said, smiling. "Particularly if his family roots are edible."

Schultz, who sensed that we were talking about him—the ham—did his party trick of staggering backwards standing on his two back paws. Nothing like a dog to warm up the atmosphere.

I had been here before, browsing in a general way, but, this time, I didn't know where to start. I was bewildered by the plethora of material.

"What do people look up here?"

"Mostly, they're interested in learning more about their family backgrounds," Hal explained. "Let me show you how it works. This isn't like a regular library where you can look up a mention of someone in books. If people weren't well known and were unlikely to have been mentioned in books, you have to search for their records in other ways.

"Suppose you wanted to find out more about your grandparents. You could start by exploring where they came from. A lot of Jewish people have grandparents who came from Eastern Europe, for example. If you had an idea when they came to the US and from where, you could try looking at shipping records or immigration records, or you might search for the records of organizations they might have belonged to, like fraternal societies, synagogues and immigrant aid groups. Even cemetery records can be useful."

He flipped through a dusty file of yellowing documents. I sneezed.

"Let's imagine your grandparents came from, oh, I don't know, say Minsk. One way of finding out more about them would be to check for Minsk *landsmanchaft* records."

"Umm... what records?" I was puzzled.

"A *landsmanshaft* is a social organization made up of people who came from the same place. They joined because they felt comfortable being with people who shared the same background. They helped each other too. It's only natural if you feel strange in a new country to want to hang out with others like yourself. If Tevye the milkman in *Fiddler on the Roof* had been a real person, he might very well have belonged to an Anatevke *landsmanshaft*. Do you see what I mean?"

I got it. "Sure. If my grandparents came from Minsk, I could find out more about them by checking the records of the Minsk *landsmanshaft*."

"That's right. But there are other ways of finding out about them too. We keep old newspapers in Yiddish, English and Hebrew, and you can sometimes find articles about the social occasions that they attended. It's kind of like detective work.

"Vatson, you amaze me."

"It's elementary, my dear Shoirlock. But there's more—a lot more here. The Archive doesn't just keep family records. We have documents, films and books about all kinds of historical things—like the World Wars, the Holocaust, and more. It attracts a lot of people from the Menorah. You'd be surprised how many residents have turned up, not to mention Sam, and, believe it or not, Ms Robins. I told you that Riva has been here often, but both your other table mates have been here too."

"That *is* hard to believe. They've never mentioned it. Pearl, no doubt," I said, "wants to prove that her antecedents were better than everyone else's, but I'm surprised that Bernice was up to it. Are you sure she wasn't looking for the bathroom? And what about Ms Robins? She's not Jewish. What on earth was she looking for?"

"She said she was interested in history. I have no reason to doubt that."

It seemed unlikely to me, but who knew?

"That's amazing," I said. "I had no idea that there was so much on record or that so many people were interested in ancient history."

Hal nodded. "It is fascinating. I love this stuff. Some people think that this is all just dead history, but it's a record of real lives. Look at this.."

He reached for a file of old newspapers, and turned the pages, brushing aside the clouds of dust that flew into the air.

"Let me find an interesting example to show you. Here, somebody has obviously been looking at this page, since it's clear of dust, so let's take it as an example. This is from a regular column called the 'Gallery of Runaway Husbands' in a national Jewish newspaper that began publication at the end of the 19th century in New York. Life was so hard for immigrants in the early days that sometimes men just left their families and disappeared. The desperate wife would sometimes advertise, like this woman, in 1924:

"I am looking for my husband, Jacob Cohen, from Propoisk, a pattern maker. He is of medium build, with a birth mark on his left arm. He abandoned me and our two children in great need. Have mercy on a Jewish mother and get in touch with Libbeh Cohen, of 4 Allen St, New York."

"Funny, the page is ripped, as if someone tried to tear it out and then stopped. I wonder why that is," he said, examining it closely.

But I was still thinking of Libbeh. "That story is so sad. I wonder if Jacob ever turned up."

"Probably not," Hal said, "but the Propoisk *landsmanshaft* society may have helped Libbeh. And in the end, her children were certainly better off in America than they were in Propoisk. Her grandchildren may well be living in luxury on Long Island today."

"I hope so," I said with a sigh. Poor Libbeh. And I complained because my table mates were less than convivial. I should count my blessings.

"But to get back to Sam, was he interested in his family records?" I asked.

"No. Actually, he said that he was interested in records of Americans who had gone to fight for the survival of the new State of Israel in the late 1940s as overseas volunteers. They were called Machal volunteers and he was one of them."

"Really?"

I was astonished—not so much that Sam had fought for Israel, but that he hadn't boasted about it. I hadn't heard a word about his exploits, and that wasn't like Sam at all. I doubted that it was true. Maybe he was trying to hide what he was really looking at.

But in any case, that didn't shed any light on why someone would want to murder him. That was a dead end, so to speak.

"Cheer up, Shoirlock," said Hal. "We'll find out who did it. I think the next step is to follow the money. Let's check out the casino."

I laughed. "Follow the money. Right. You sound like an FBI agent. Are you sure you don't have anything undercover in your own history?"

"Nope. I'm just a retired teacher from Florida with an interest in genealogy. My wife died four years ago and I found it was just too depressing living in the same place without her. My daughter lives in Aurora, and this seemed the obvious place to start again, so I rented an apartment near her and here I am. Between my family, my dog and this volunteer job, I've managed to make a new life for myself, of sorts. It's lonely sometimes, but I keep busy."

"So you're not a plastic surgeon gone bad, or a white collar criminal just released from prison?"

"Nothing that interesting," he said, grinning. "Why would you think so?

"It's the Menorah gossip mill. Pearl and Mollie between them have manufactured quite a story about why you came to live in Aurora."

"Well, I won't disillusion them. I kind of like the thought of being a released con, hiding millions."

He looked at me keenly. "But what about you? Why did you decide to live here?"

"My story isn't very different," I said. "My husband died a few years ago too, and because I have asthma and my son was worried about me living on my own, he insisted that I move into the Menorah. He pays for it too. I love to bake, so I keep busy helping out in the kitchen, even though that pisses off Ms Robins. And I have to admit, this murder, if that's what it is, is the most exciting thing to have happened since I moved in."

"Exciting, yes, but dangerous too. Don't forget, if there really is a murderer—and I'm not at all sure that there is—there may be a homicidal maniac around."

I shrugged. "Why would he trouble with me? Anyway, I have

this guy to protect me. Right, Schultzie?"

Schultz barked, right on cue.

"He, or she, might figure that you're on his trail and try to stop you," Hal said.

"I'm not worried."

Hal looked at me intently. "But I am."

Schultz lifted his leg near a pile of papers, interrupting this fascinating discussion.

"Get him out of here! Quick!"

"I'm going," I said, scooping up Schultz. The discussion would have to wait.

✦ Chapter Eleven ✦

The Menorah mini bus left for the Pink Flamingo Casino, which was on the outskirts of Aurora, every Friday at 10 am and came back late in the afternoon. If you were interested in a day's fun losing money, you could sign up at the front desk for a place in the bus. It was a popular day trip and seats filled up quickly. Riva and I had signed up early to make sure of finding a place.

Hal was meeting us at the Casino. He had offered to drive us, but we didn't want to generate more gossip than was absolutely necessary. Fat chance.

It didn't take long. Mollie, who was also going, spied us in the queue.

"Where are you going, Ellie? Are you coming with us to the casino? You don't usually come. And Riva too? And the dog?" She chuckled. She obviously thought the idea of Riva, with her orthopedic oxfords and general air of disapproval celebrating a winning blackjack hand was amusing. I had to stifle a smile myself at the thought.

Mollie didn't give me a chance to reply, but no answer was needed: she pushed her walker with great haste to the Vintage Cafe coffee shop, no doubt to spread the word. Ms Robins, who could see the action from her office, also seemed to be paying close attention.

I loved this! Nobody had ever gossiped about me before. My star was rising.

Mollie had dressed for the occasion in a bright red muu-muu, with matching lipstick. Her eye makeup had also been carefully applied, although slathered on might be a more truthful description. She had penciled in one eyebrow above her normal one. It gave her a rakish look, like a demented pirate.

"Let's go! I know I'm going to be lucky today," she cackled, as she climbed unsteadily into the waiting bus.

"Do you play blackjack?" I asked her.

"No, that was Sam's game. I play the nickel slots. When I lose $20, I stop. But I bet I win today."

I admired her optimism. Not too many 93-year-olds were so up for adventure.

"I hope you do win," I told her.

Mollie, along with all the others, was in an upbeat mood. Nobody actually expected to hit the jackpot, but for their small investment, they knew they would have the fun and the excitement of trying. And who knew? Everyone remembered the time last year when Bernice had fed a quarter into a slot machine and won $400. Wow! That was excitement. For a while after that, demand had been high to sign up for the mini-bus to the casino. Then Bernice got overconfident, lost the stratospheric sum of $50 and the excitement petered out.

As we were about to get into the mini-bus, a car drew up and to my astonishment, my son Josh got out, carrying an overnight bag. He hadn't been kidding about checking up on me, but I hadn't thought that it would be so soon. Now what was I going to do?

"Mom, where are you going?" he said, with an incredulous look at Mollie.

I gave him a quick hug. "I'm sorry I can't stay right now, but I'll be back in a few hours. You can wait in my suite." I tossed him my keys. "We're going to the casino."

"The casino? I didn't know you gambled." Josh looked dazed. "What's happened to you?"

"Nothing! I'm fine," I said, waving blithely, as the mini-bus set off. "See you soon."

I looked back. Josh was still standing there, his mouth gaping open. There was going to be hell to pay, unless I could think of a way to get out of it. But in the meantime, I had other things on my mind. Hal was waiting!

At the casino, the blinking lights and the ding of slot machines momentarily dazzled me. Hey, what the heck. I reached into my purse for a quarter and stuck it into the "Red Hot Devil", a tempting slot machine, which ate my quarter and brought me back to reality.

Riva looked at me disapprovingly. "We are here to find out about Sam, not gamble, "she said in her usual chiding tone. "Gambling is for fools. Where is Hal?" She looked around, taking in the flashing lights, the clatter of pinball machines and lack of windows in the vast hall. You wouldn't know if it were day or night here. No doubt that was the aim.

Riva was definitely getting antsy. I had the feeling that if I got up to any more mischief, Riva would take away my privileges. Or maybe give me detention.

"Riva, did you ever work as a teacher by chance?"

"Yes, in fact I was the assistant principal of a girl's school before my marriage. How did you know?"

"Oh," I said innocently. "I just guessed."

Hal rushed up to us, patted Schultz and gave us each a high five.

"Ok, team. Let's start detecting. How should we go about this?"

"Mollie said that Sam used to play blackjack, so maybe we could start by asking the blackjack dealers if they knew him," I suggested. "Let's split up and each take a different table."

"I don't know how to play," said Riva. She seemed proud of the fact.

"Then come with me," Hal told her.

Twenty minutes later, we met glumly. None of us had got a word out of the croupiers, except for what related to the game. What a bunch of spoilsports. I had lost $10 and Hal hadn't done much better. In fact, he and Riva had been asked to leave because the dog was distracting gamblers at the table. So what now?

"I'll try asking at the office if they knew Sam," Hal declared. "Come along, Riva. Maybe you'll intimidate them into telling us something."

"I do not intimidate," she said sternly.

Hal winked at me.

"Good luck at the office. I'm going to get something to eat," I said. Well, it had been a long time since breakfast. Ok, it had been two hours, but I had to keep my strength up, right?

The bar wasn't exactly a gastronomic haven—it was more of a pit stop—but it did offer coffee and cellophane-wrapped pastries. The bartender was chatty and obviously bored as he wiped the bar with a dingy cloth.

"This is my first time here," I offered.

"Yes? Well, I hope you break the bank." He refilled my coffee cup. "Not that that's very likely."

"Well, some people do win. I had a friend who used to come here all the time. He was lucky. Maybe you knew him? His name was Sam Levin."

"An old guy with black hair? Yeah, I knew him. But I wouldn't call him lucky. Every time he lost, he would order a Jack Daniels and cry on my shoulder. And he went through a lot of Jack Daniels. I heard that he lost big."

Really? That was just the proof I wanted to hear. Hurriedly, I paid for my coffee and rushed out to find Hal and Riva and share my news. I found them outside the office.

"The bartender told me that Sam was a big loser," I said eagerly. "So where did he get the money? He must have been blackmailing someone, for sure."

"Yes, that is convincing," Riva nodded. "Our next step is to discover who he was blackmailing, and why."

"Hey, hang on," said Hal. "This has been fun, but you two don't want to get involved in anything dangerous. I think we should tell the police and let them deal with it."

"I'm not going to tell the police," I said firmly. "The police don't think he was murdered. They think I'm just an old bat who watches too much television and bakes brownies. If we tell them about Hal's gambling and his money, they'll want to know how we discovered he had money in his room. We'll be in trouble and they'll just forget the whole thing about Sam."

I stared at Riva and Hal. "I vote that we investigate more. Are you in or not?"

"Certainly I am in," said Riva firmly. Schultz barked, right on cue.

"This is not going to be easy," Hal said dubiously. "And it could be trouble."

"What? Are you giving up already?"

"And leave you two reckless idiots to your own devices? Nope, I'll go along, if only to keep an eye on you."

"That is more like it," Riva said.

❧ Chapter Twelve ❧

Sam was blackmailing someone who might have killed him. That much we were sure of—at least Riva and I were sure of— but who was the villain? And what was the motive? I was confused.

It was time to explore the sex angle, odd though it was to think of Sam, the octogenarian, being overcome by passion. I suspected it was all just talk with him. But on the other hand, with modern medicine, anything was possible. I would start, of course, with the Menorah gossip mill.

But meanwhile, my son was a complication. Josh was staying with me and showing no signs of leaving. I had heard him talking on the phone to my daughter Tami, telling her that I apparently had become a gambler, and he was planning to stick around to find out what my mental state was.

Normally, I would have been over the moon with joy at a visit from my son, but right now, his stay was a complication. Josh would have to be kept in the dark about the doings at the Menorah and my involvement and that wasn't going to be easy. Josh was sharp!

Although it would have made it easier if he had gone to stay in a nearby hotel, I couldn't really suggest it, and since he wanted to stay as close to me as possible, Josh had chosen to share my suite and sleep on the pull-out bed in my living room. That was a sacrifice I appreciated. But though he was willing to put up with the sleeping arrangements, uncomfortable as they were, after the first meal, he drew the line at eating in the dining room. He was the kind of snobby eater who preferred fish quenelles to gefilte fish, but that wasn't the reason. It wasn't the food that irritated him so much as the fact that a lot of the residents homed in on a nice, Jewish, available young man and drove him crazy by pestering him to meet their granddaughters. When he said that he wasn't in the market for a wife, they just tried harder.

Mollie was typical. Subtle she wasn't. On a previous visit, she had once caught us on the way to breakfast and forced him to join her on the sofa in the entrance hall. Josh was smart enough to run a company, but even he was no match for Mollie and so he had sat down beside her.

Mollie didn't waste time on small talk.

"You should meet my granddaughter Jill," she had said. "What a beauty! And smart too. She's tops in her class and the way she skates—like Sonya Henie. I could introduce you."

"Mollie, Jill is 16 years old," I had said, embarrassed. "Josh isn't a cradle robber. Anyway, Josh has never heard of Sonya Henie. I think she skated in the 1930s."

"So she's dead. So what? Jill skates better than her anyway. Anyway, in four years, Jill will be 20. That's too young? Of course not! By the way, how much did you say you earned, Josh?"

No, Josh was not going to let himself in for that again. He had begged me to come with him to a nice restaurant for lunch, but I had refused. Josh couldn't believe this—he knew how much I loved good food. I was afraid he was getting suspicious. Either that, or he was becoming convinced I was beginning to lose all my marbles. Or both.

It gave me a pang to give up a nice lunch, especially since Josh was a *feinschmecker*—a fussy gourmet—for whom nothing but the best food and wine would do, but I knew there would be other opportunities. And I had to find out who Sam was blackmailing.

Our first prospective source was Pearl. She had hinted that Sam was having an affair. Could that be true? And if so, how did she know?

At lunch, I brought up the subject. It wasn't hard to introduce since the two deaths were the main topics of conversation at every table. Maurice's departure had given Pearl something legitimate to gripe about and she was enjoying every minute. Before the first course had been brought around, she had started kvetching.

"I see they haven't replaced Maurice yet. No wonder the service is so slow," she said, looking around for a waiter. "You'd think Ms. Robins could have hired somebody to replace Maurice."

"Give Ms. Robins a chance," I said. "It's only been a few days. The poor guy has just been buried."

I put down my fork and changed the subject.

"Pearl, what did you mean when you said the other day that Sam was having an affair with somebody here? With who? How do you know?"

"An affair?" Bernice perked up her ears. She had selective hearing. Anything to do with sex or bathrooms, she picked up.

"I don't know who the woman was," Pearl admitted, "but I do know that he was involved with someone. Mollie said so and she hears everything. She said that Sam boasted that he met women on the JLove internet dating site and some of them lived here. He went on about how they were fighting over him, and what a great lover he was. Not only that; Mollie saw him talking to Ms Robins and she said that Ms. Robins looked very excited. She figured that she was one of his lovers."

I burst out laughing. "Ms. Robins! I can't imagine anything more unlikely than her being attracted to Sam, unless it's him being attracted to her. Really, Pearl. You have more sense than to believe a story like that."

Pearl was miffed. "Well, it's not as if there are so many men around here to choose from. I wouldn't be surprised if one of the women he was involved with murdered him, out of jealousy. Why not Ms. Robins?"

"Much as I wouldn't mind seeing Ms. Robins hauled away in shackles, you have to admit she's the last person anyone would suspect. She's reasonably attractive and she's more than 30 years younger than Sam was. Isn't she married, anyway?"

"Divorced. She doesn't wear a wedding ring."

"And that's all the evidence you have? Couldn't Mollie come up with something better than a scenario where Ms Robins connected with Sam on the internet, had mad sex with him and then murdered him out of jealousy because he was involved with some other octogenarian resident?"

Bernice was listening with interest, and a certain amount of bewilderment.

"Sam was having sex with Ms Robins?"

I sighed. "No Bernice. She was not."

"He's dead now." She said it with a certain amount of satisfaction. Could Bernice...? No. Not even Mollie would believe that. Even Schultz would be a more likely candidate for a murderer.

But the sex angle had to be checked, and the best place for that, short of inspecting bedrooms, was the computer in the library. There was no way we could get into his room again to use Sam's own computer, and anyway, his room had probably been emptied by now. I would try to have another look at Sam's JLove account. But how could I do that? Even though the computer screen usually opened directly to the JLove site, because that was what people looked at most, we didn't know Sam's password.

Ever the optimist, I decided to fool around with the computer, just in case a miracle happened and I could get into Sam's account. It would have to be late at night, which around here meant after 9 pm. Most residents were asleep by then. (I usually was myself, so I would have to take some sustenance, in the form of cookies, to keep awake.) Riva would come too.

Fortunately, Josh wouldn't have come back from dinner yet. He liked to eat fashionably late, which was another reason he didn't care to join us in the Menorah dining room. Six o'clock for him was time for a coffee break, not supper. No doubt he had found some attractive woman to accompany him, as a substitute for me. Josh was a heartbreaker. I wondered who he would eventually choose to marry, assuming he ever did.

By 8:45, I was ready. I knocked on Riva's door, and the two of us crept quietly to the library.

Sam's grandson Noah was on the computer, playing some noisy game. His spiky black hair now had red streaks. I hoped it wouldn't give Mollie ideas.

"What are you doing here, Noah? Hasn't your family left yet?"

"Nope. We have to clean out Zaidie's room, so we're spending a week in a guest suite."

He popped his gum. Riva winced.

"That must be boring for you." I smiled.

"Yeah. My IPad is broken and like, all these old dudes hang around the computer so I can't even get near it. All they want to do is look at a dating site. Gross."

I had a thought. I remembered Sam had claimed that what he was researching in the Community Archive was the Machal group of American volunteers who had fought in Israel and which he had claimed he belonged to. Noah might know.

"Noah, do you happen to know if your grandfather ever went to Israel when he was young?"

Noah looked blank. "Nah, he never visited Israel. He didn't like to fly any further than Miami."

Just as I thought. Sam had made that up. There was something else he was looking up in the Community Archive; something he wanted to remain secret. Riva nodded at me thoughtfully. Then she changed the subject. Maybe Noah could be useful. Maybe he could help us see what Sam was up to on his romantic social sites.

"Could you get into your grandfather's JLove account, young man?" she asked.

"Sure. I know his login. He used the same password for everything, so he wouldn't forget it—'SamtheMan'. What a dope."

Then he gave me a sideways look.

"What do you want it for? Hey, I bet you figure he was killed and you want to find out who had it in for him. Right?"

The kid was craftier than he looked.

"I could help." His eyes sparkled and I swear his pimples reddened in excitement.

"I play 'Evil Genius' all the time. It's all about spies and murder and world domination. This murder is nothing compared to that. I could easily solve it. I hear everything people say and nobody pays attention to me. I could pick up a lot of information. Hey, shit, I could get with the program."

Riva frowned. "Please watch your language," she told him.

"Hey, chill, Bubbie." He popped his gum again.

Riva was so startled at this insubordination that she was momentarily struck dumb—fortunately for Noah. He had yet to learn how intimidating she could be.

In spite of what an irritating kid he was, I had to admit that Noah might certainly be useful. Of course, we would have to keep him out of trouble, but if he just restricted himself to helping with the computer and listening to what people said, I didn't think that he would be in any danger. I had to admit, I was glad that Hal wasn't around. I suspected he might not approve of the newest member of the team.

"What do you think, Riva?" I asked.

She nodded thoughtfully. "I think Noah could be helpful, if he wants to. And if he learns to speak respectfully and to spit out his gum. My name is Mrs. Mannheim, Noah. I am not your Bubbie."

Riva may have been only five foot nothing in height, but there was something about her that made an impression even on Noah. He looked startled, removed his gum and stuck it to the underside of the computer screen. Riva raised her eyebrows and glared. Abashed, Noam removed the gum and swallowed it. I sighed. This boy was going to be a trial. I hoped involving him was worth it.

Schultz barked. I swear, that dog understood everything. He seemed to be voting to include Noah. So be it.

Our motley detective crew now consisted of two ladies of advanced age, one retired librarian, a kid with a dirty mouth and a dog. What a team!

"OK, you're in," I said. "The first thing we need is a list of the women that your Zaidie was messaging.

"Cool!"

We huddled over his shoulder to watch as he clicked away at the computer. The kid was impressive. I still hadn't mastered Skype, let alone the complications of JLove. I could just about manage to find Google.

Ten minutes later, Noah leaned back with a grin of satisfaction. "OK. Here's what I've got. He's been sending messages to dozens of women, but only two have answered. One's in Canada and one is Joyce, but he didn't answer her. Horny old goat."

"That is no way to talk about your grandfather," said Riva, to no effect.

"And that's all?" I asked. "No one else here? What about Ms. Robins?"

"Nope. Oh, here. There's also that old bird who sits in the lobby. She's been sending him messages using her real name, but he ignores them. I guess she didn't realize that the guy she's been messaging is Sam."

Riva snorted. "The picture he's using is so ancient that no wonder she didn't recognize him."

"It works both ways," I said, laughing. "Look at the picture she posted. She looks like Betty Grable."

I peered closer. "It *is* Betty Grable. This photograph must have been taken in the 1940s! Mollie didn't have enough computer smarts to know that you shouldn't use your real name with a phony picture if you want to fool men."

"I notice she's also taken 40 years off her age," I added.

I rubbed my forehead. "Unfortunately, this leaves us back where we started. Sam certainly wasn't having an affair with anyone he met on JLove, which is not to say that he wasn't having an affair with someone he knew here. Log out; there's something I want to check. Come with me."

We headed back to my suite, passing through the lobby on the way. Mollie had gone to bed, but Ms. Robins, who was still in her office, gave us a suspicious look. Good grief, did the woman live here? I was tempted to stick out my tongue, but restrained myself.

In the room, I dug out the three packages of Viagra I had found in Sam's bathroom. Noah and Riva crowded around to look. I gasped.

"What?" said Noah.

"Look at the expiration dates on the pill boxes," I said. And there they were—July 1999, April 2002 and November 2004. Not only that, but not a single pill had been taken out of the package.

If Sam had ever been having an affair, it had taken place back in the mists of history. He was a fake. There was no jealous lover because Sam wasn't sleeping with anyone at all.

❧ Chapter Thirteen ❧

Hal would want to know about this, so I visited the Community Archive again the next day early, before Josh woke up, with a box of freshly-baked rugelach cookies. I took along Schulz. Hal wasn't thrilled at the inclusion of Noah in our increasingly ill-assorted detective circle—("Schultz, ok, but Noah, uh-uh")—on the grounds that the kid was foolhardy and would get himself into trouble, but the atmosphere lightened when I told him about our discoveries.

He smiled at the story of Mollie, aka Betty Grable, and burst into laughter when I got to the part about the expired Viagra.

"Poor guy!" he said. "He was just a dreamer."

I liked the fact that Hal sympathized with Sam, rather than making fun of him. Hal was a *mensch*, no doubt about it. A *mensch* is the Yiddish term for a person of integrity; someone who is responsible; who knows right from wrong; a good guy. He's someone people can look up to. That was Hal to a T—at least in my book.

I curled up in an oversized cracked leather armchair, Schultz in my lap and a coffee cup beside me. Outside, a winter storm was hurling snow at the window, but inside, in the warm, stuffy atmosphere of the archive, with its clutter of books and files, coffee cups and musty papers, it was comfortably cozy. The past seemed to meld with the present, as if the men and women who had once lived still lingered here. As long as this Community Archive existed, they would, in a sense, exist too. There was a sense of continuity in the room.

I remembered the story of Libbeh, and I wondered again what had happened to her. When I had time, I thought, I would see if there was something in the Community Archive that might give a clue as to whether her story had a happy ending. Surely Hal must know how to find out.

"I really like this place," I mused. "There's something meaningful about it. It's filled with the ghosts of the people who came before us, like Libbeh, but it's not sad or scary. It's as if the people here want us to hear their stories. Do you think we could find out what happened to Libbeh?

"I suppose we can try, if you're interested. We'll give it a go next week."

I took another sip of hot coffee and snuggled deeper into the chair.

"No wonder so many people hang out here. Didn't you say that a lot of the residents of the Menorah have come to the Community Archive to look up stuff?"

"Sure. I told you—lots. Sam for one, even Ms Robins. She said she wanted to learn more about local Jewish history, because a lot of the people at the Menorah or their families are mentioned in the records, so I showed her the files of Jewish newspapers. You'd be surprised how many people have an interest in history."

"I'm sure Riva does. She's lived through history, but I can't imagine that most of the residents have the same interest. Most of them seem to be mainly interested in gossip and their aches and pains. That's what they talk about anyway."

"You'd be surprised. I keep a log of who visits. Take a look," said Hal, opening a binder on his desk.

He was right; I was surprised. There were daily lists of visitors, and the numbers were way higher than I had imagined. Some names I didn't recognize. I assumed they were from the city. Others were indeed from the Menorah. Among them were a number of most unlikely history lovers, including Pearl and Bernice.

"Pearl is proud of how rich and important her family was and no doubt wanted to preen a bit, but Bernice? Maybe she was following Pearl. Maybe she was looking for the bathroom again and wandered off course."

"Maybe you've underestimated your friends," Hal said.

I smiled to myself. Hal was so innocent. There was, of course, another reason they might have visited the Community Archive. They wanted an excuse to chat to Hal!

Like me.

"It's not just the history that makes this place so interesting to me," I said. "I just have a feeling that the Community Archive might be connected in some ways to the murders. After all, Sam hung out here. Maybe he found something he could connect to blackmail."

Hal wrinkled his brow quizzically. "Blackmail material? Here? Look around. There's nothing but old papers and books. How could any of this be linked to murder? What could Sam have possibly found out about anybody that would be blackmail material? That they belonged to the Youth Choir of Petropopoik in 1928? That they attended the annual dinner of the Etz Chaim synagogue? You've got quite an imagination, Shoirlock. Anyway, Maurice never came here, so there's no connection at all to his death."

True.

Hal took off his glasses, gave them a polish, and then looked at me.

"Ellie, I think you're getting over-involved here. I've said this before: this isn't a television program; these may be real murders. I think you should leave solving the crime, if there is a crime, up to the police."

"But the police don't take us seriously. You saw for yourself how they treated me. They think that because the residents here are old, they're incapable of feeling normal human emotions, let alone killing somebody. They don't even think that Sam and Maurice were murdered. I just know that they're being too dismissive."

"Maybe they are, but you seem to forget that you have asthma. Stress can bring on an attack, and I can't think of anything more stressful than dealing with a homicidal maniac. I just don't want you to get sick."

Punching me gently on the arm, Hal said, "You're going to get in trouble. I want you to promise me that you won't go looking for a murderer. Agreed?"

I frowned. I liked Hal a lot, but this was a little too bossy for my taste. I had been married to a guy who routinely assumed he was the one to make decisions in the family. My two kids were prone to order me around too. I had gone along with it, but now that I was on my own, I had grown used to making my own decisions, and I liked that freedom. I didn't appreciate Hal bringing up the fact that I had asthma either. I wasn't incapacitated. I carried my inhaler with me all the time and it had never failed to stop an attack.

On the other hand... it was lovely to have someone worry about me. Nice guys like Hal are pretty rare. He liked me and he wanted me to be safe. Is that so terrible? What, was I crazy, to throw that away, just for a little adventure?

I guess I was. And also stubborn, and unwilling to let murderers get away with their crimes.

"Promise," I agreed, with my fingers crossed behind my back. OK, it wasn't exactly what I intended. And it wasn't what he thought I intended.

Pants on fire. (Well, a little white lie never hurt anyone. Or so I hoped.)

❧ ❦

At dinner that night, the dining room looked half deserted. It was pathetic—with Maurice missing, half the pep seemed to have left the room. A lot of the residents seemed to have opted to eat in their rooms. Those still dining here seemed listless.

"I knew it," Pearl announced. "People are leaving. Joyce told me this morning that she was going to look for someplace else to live and Mollie said that Ms Robins has been mobbed by people wanting to move."

"Leaving? I'm not leaving," said Bernice, who looked, as usual, confused.

"Well, maybe you should," Pearl responded. "My daughter is very insistent that I move in with her. Her husband is a doctor, you know."

"Yes, we know," said Riva sharply. "A Jewish doctor, as you've told us many times."

Pearl was put out. She snapped back, "Maybe you should think about getting out of here too. I wouldn't rely on your yappy dog to protect you if a murderer comes around to your suite."

She got up from the table. "Come on, Bernice. Let's find better company."

Trailing Bernice, Queen Pearl swept out of the room. That was fine with me; I had lots to talk about with Riva.

Pushing my plate aside, I whispered, "Hey, I have an idea. The sex angle turned out to be a bust, but that leaves us with blackmail as a motive. Sam had to be blackmailing someone; otherwise where would he get all that cash? I think a prime suspect has to be Ms. Robins. She had the opportunity; she could easily find out what pills Sam was taking and she's so mysterious that she's probably hiding something shady."

Riva looked skeptical, but she tried to be open-minded.

"You may be right, but can we possibly find out what her secret is, if she does have one?

"I think we have to start with her office."

Riva laughed. "I think we would be hard put to find her out of the office. And she locks it every night."

"She has to go home sometime," I said. "Maybe we could cook up a story so that Katerine would let us in."

"That is unlikely. Katerine is not a fool and she would not want to get fired. I have a better idea." She reached in her handbag for her wallet and pulled out a credit card.

"You're going to hire a house breaker and pay with a credit card?" I was astonished.

"No. Don't be ridiculous Ellie. I am going to use this card to open the lock on the door. It's not a complicated lock. Any fool could do this."

She looked at me as if to indicate that even a fool like me could manage it. I shook my head. "You're full of wonders, Riva. Truly, you're a genuine, Ms.Marplestein. Where did you learn this trick? No, don't tell me. Probably better if I don't know."

Riva put her credit card back in her purse. "We will do it tonight, but we will leave Noah out of it. Schultz will protect us."

❧ Chapter Fourteen ❧

How was I going to keep Josh from knowing what we intended? That was a problem. I thought about it and came up with a plan. I would tell Josh that I wanted to go out with him for dinner. Then, after dinner, I would tell him that I was tired and ask him to bring me home. Judging from his usual habits, he would drop me off and then go out somewhere on his own. Retiring for the night at 9:30 pm, as I did, wasn't exactly his style. By the time he got home from wherever he had gone, we would have done the dirty deed and I would be back in my own bed, innocent as could be. Genius!

It worked like a charm.

"Let's go out for dinner this evening," I suggested.

"You want to? You mean that you don't want to eat brisket and knishes in the dining room in the company of Pearl and Bernice? I don't believe it."

Josh liked teasing me, but I wasn't pleased about him insulting my knishes. (The Menorah's brisket, on the other hand, he was welcome to insult.) But I let it go.

"What kind of meal do you feel like, Mom? Italian? Chinese?"

"You choose," I told him. "As long as I get to drink a Mojito in place of the ice water we get here."

"You can drink anything you want," he said fondly.

Josh can be very sweet sometimes.

We opted for Japanese—I love sushi—and as we settled down that evening at a table at Yakimono, the fanciest Japanese restaurant in town, I realized this was the first time in months that I had had Josh to myself. This was a bigger treat even than tempura. I knew better than to let anything drop about the murders, but maybe I could just hint a little about Hal. First though, I would pump Josh about himself. Hey, I'm a mother.

"Josh, how are things going?" I began.

"Great," he said. "I'm working on a deal with a company in South Korea. If it comes off, our firm will make a fortune."

"You know that's not what I meant. Are you seeing someone? Sweetie, you're in your 40's now. It's time you settled down. I read in the paper that your sperm gets old and you can't have babies anymore after a certain age. Don't you want children?"

"Mom, would you lay off? You have grandchildren. Tami has kids. There's plenty of time. It's complete nonsense about sperm getting old. Where did you read that? A tabloid?"

Actually, I had indeed read it in one of Mollie's tabloids, but I wasn't going to admit it. I attacked Josh from another angle.

"Have you ever heard of JLove?" I asked, changing the subject.

"Yes, I have, and I'm not interested. Where did you hear about JLove? You shouldn't be fooling around with that kind of site. By the way, I found some Viagra pills in the bathroom this morning. Surely you aren't involved with any of the *alte kakers* in the Menorah? Or are you?"

He looked as if he couldn't decide if this were a joke or not.

"No, of course I'm not fooling around. The Viagra is out of date anyway. I found it in Sam's bathroom and took it away so that his family wouldn't be embarrassed."

"What? That guy you told me about who died last week? What were you doing in his bathroom? Mom, what's going on? What are you getting up to?"

"I'm not getting up to anything," I said with all the dignity I could muster. "I was helping his family clean his suite, that's all."

Josh looked at me suspiciously, and we spent the rest of the meal talking about the new deal that was going to make him a fortune. Another fortune, that is, in addition to the one he already had. I didn't bother to tell him about Hal. I didn't have the nerve, since he had discovered Viagra in my bathroom and might jump to conclusions. How embarrassing would that be!

It was late when we got back but Josh told me that he was going out to a club and would be back late.

"Throw out the Viagra," was his parting shot.

๛ ๛

I'm not a person who stays up late. On the contrary, I'm usually nodding off by 9, and this was the second night in a week that I'd had to stay up late. On the other hand, I tend to bounce out of bed at 6 am, ready for my coffee and the morning paper. It used to drive my late husband crazy. He was a night bird and loved to sleep in the morning. With our two conflicting schedules, sometimes we spent time together only at suppertime. To tell the truth, that wasn't always something I regretted too much. He was a difficult guy.

By the time Riva knocked on my door at midnight, I was fast asleep on the sofa, with the TV on. Fortunately, Josh was still out, getting up to God only knew what.

Riva had no mercy. "Wake up!" she said, shaking me." We must go now."

Schultz licked my face. That woke me up all right, and not in a good way.

"Get off me, you silly pooch," I said, grimacing, rising painfully from the sofa. It's not so easy to raise yourself from a low couch at my age. I needed some reviving.

"What about a snack before we go?" I asked hopefully, thinking of the left-over rugelach in the cookie container.

"Is food all you think about?"asked Riva. She sounded exasperated. I was hurt. Is there something wrong with thinking about food?

"No. I think about lots of things," I said in an injured tone, "but maybe food too." I had to be honest. "So, are we going to have a snack, for energy?"

"No!" Riva may have been five foot nothing, but she knew something about giving orders. If she were on the trail of the murderer, I wouldn't give two cents for his—or her—chances.

Schultz looked downcast. He understood. I snuck him another one of the rugelach when Riva's back was turned. It was my own private rebellious gesture against her bossiness.

"I saw that," she said. But she said it with a small smile.

The lobby, at this unholy hour, was of course deserted. There was a security guy on the premises, but he usually wandered around outside if he wasn't dozing off by the door. (The problem was, of course, that in Minnesota, you didn't wander around for very long outside in winter. He would be coming in again soon, no doubt.)

There was no doorman. All the residents had front door keys, so there was no need for someone to let them in. The only sound was the crackling of the imitation logs in the gas fireplace. Still, we felt as if we had to whisper.

I frowned at Schultz. "No barking!" He wagged his tail, but refrained from yapping. I knew he understood, but I still didn't trust him.

"Was it really necessary to bring the dog, Riva?"

"Of course. He will warn us if anyone comes. If that happens, we will leave the office and pretend we couldn't sleep."

It occurred to me that Riva had some personality traits in common with Ms. Robins, different as they were in other essentials. If either of them ever warmed up a little, they might even improve the place. But no—I loved Riva, and just couldn't like Ms. Robins, whose mean streak was all too often in evidence. I had to admit that none of us would be too sad if she turned out to be the murderer. But was that just wishful thinking?

At the door of the office, Riva pulled out her credit card and slipped it between the door jamb and the door, just below the lock. Then she bent her card, and wiggled it. Nothing happened, except that the card bent out of shape.

"Tsk," she muttered and tried again. Not surprisingly, the lock popped open. Even inanimate objects seemed to give way before our intimidating Riva.

The office was as bare and uninviting by night as it was by day. The desk drawers were locked, but the file cabinet looked open.

"Work your credit card magic on the desk drawers," I said. Riva took out her card, now the worse for wear, and wiggled it around in the top drawer until the lock popped open.

Nothing of any interest presented itself. Makeup, wet wipes, paper clips and other supplies, all in immaculate order. Bo-ring, as Noah would say. The other drawers were just as impersonal.

"What now?"

"The filing cabinet," said Riva.

At first glance, that seemed even less promising—just row after row of files. There were files on personnel, files on financial matters and on administrative matters. That seemed to be all.

"There's nothing scandalous here at all," I said, disappointed.

"What did you expect, Ellie?" Riva said acerbically. "A file titled 'Murderers in Residence" or maybe "'Look in here to find out who did it?'"

I ignored her. Then I looked again. I pulled out a file marked "Correspondence." The top letter was from the firm that owned the Menorah Residence. I skimmed it quickly: it seemed that Ms. Robins' job was on the line. The Menorah wasn't full and it was losing money. Ms. Robins was ordered to cut expenses and do what she could to entice new residents.

That made me think.

"It certainly wasn't in Ms. Robins' interest to have Sam and Maurice knocked off. On the contrary; the murders make people leave, rather than move in. That seems to let her off the hook."

"I am not sure that is correct," said Riva. "She might have such a strong reason for murder that it would overcome any risks to her job. She must be very nervous, anyway. But there is nothing here. Let's go."

Not so fast. I thought of all the fascinating stuff there might be in the personnel files. Call me inquisitive—ok call me nosy, but I had to have a look.

I picked up Ms. Robins' own personnel file and swiftly skimmed over her resume. As expected, she had sterling qualifications—two university degrees followed by a course in Hotel Management and jobs at various institutions around the country. Her references were equally impressive. She'd moved around a lot though. I wondered why.

But where was the good stuff? I looked for personal details. Hmm... born in—well, well, she was older than I thought. Married to John Robins 15 years ago, and divorced 10 years later. One child. One child? There were no pictures of a child around her office, and as far as I knew, she had never mentioned offspring. When did she have time for a child, anyway, since she practically lived here? Maiden name—Klara Grobel. *Klara Grobel?* I was stunned.

"Come, Ellie!" Riva pulled my arm. "Are you poking your nose where it doesn't belong again? This is not relevant to us."

"You said that about Sam's stuff too, and look what we learned," I said, shaking my arm free impatiently. "You won't believe what I just read!"

Then, just as I was about to share my great find, Schultz barked. The front door swung open and George, the security guy, entered the lobby. He hadn't seen us yet. Riva, with her walker, moved faster than I would have thought possible out of the office and into the lobby. I was slower on the uptake; I crouched down behind the desk, which was about all I could do under the circumstances, and grimaced as my knees protested.

I trusted Riva to get us out of this. If anyone could do it, she could. And as usual, I was impressed by her competence. From a brisk golden ager to an old, limping lady was the work of a moment. She leaned on her walker, and moaned. Well, it had worked with Katerine.

"What are you doing here, Mrs. Mannheim?" asked George.

"Oy," she sighed. "I could not sleep with the pain of my arthritis. You youngsters don't understand such things." She looked up into his eyes, with the expression of a wounded deer.

That was a good touch. George was 60 if he was a day. He would like being called a youngster.

In a gentle tone, George said, "Let me help you back to your room. I know it's hard for you to move around." He put his arm around her.

Yes! I thought. Help her back to her room and get the heck out of here so I can get up. Assuming I can. This crouching position was doing nothing for my sacroiliac. But would George notice the open office door? I held my breath.

Drat. He did.

"Ms. Robins has left her office door open. That isn't like her. I'll just lock it," he said.

I was alarmed. That meant that in the best case scenario, even if George didn't see me, Riva would have to find some way to come back and let me out with her crumpled credit card. Either that, or Ms. Robins would find me in the morning, and I hated to think what that would mean. At the very least, it would mean missing breakfast. That was bad news.

But it didn't come to that.

The dog, once again, did me in.

Up to now, Schultz had been standing guard in the lobby. But now, with his mistress in the care of George, he figured his job was over and we were all playing hide and seek. Tail wagging, he trotted into the office through the open door, skirted round the desk and woofed happily, as if to say, "I found you. That was fun!"

George pulled out a gun and strode into the office.

I raised my arms and grinned foolishly. All I could think of to say was "It's a fair cop." That's what guilty people say in British detective dramas when someone has caught them doing something wrong. But I guess George didn't watch British shows.

"Huh? What on earth are you doing here, Mrs. Shapiro?"

I was at a loss. So was Riva, for once. The only one who knew what to do was Schultz, who went straight for my pocket, where, as it happened, I had a few more rugelach.

"Ellie!" Riva said. "You had to bring cookies?"

"So where's the harm in a little midnight snack?"

Riva rolled her eyes. George, meanwhile, was not amused.

"I don't know what you ladies think you're doing in a private office, but whatever it is, it's illegal."

"You're not going to tell Ms. Robins are you?" I pleaded.

"Of course I am. And I'm also going to tell the police. This is breaking and entering. And don't give me more of your nonsense," he added to Riva, who was groaning and limping again in a last-ditch effort to influence him.

I could deal with the police, but the thought of Ms. Robins finding out was horrific. The thought of Josh learning about my late night escapade was even worse. Hal would hear about it too. I'd promised him to stay out of trouble, and I'd lied. He wasn't going to like it.

I reached for my inhaler, just in case.

❧ Chapter Fifteen ❧

I was locked in a cage, but where this was, I couldn't tell. A chandelier dangled from the top of the cage, and when I looked closely, I saw that it was made of credit cards, sharpened like blades. A dog barked in the distance.

"Schultz!" I called out weakly. "Save me." The barks died away, and then, the revolving blades began sinking, approaching closer. I lay on the floor of the cage, with my arms around my head.

"Help!" It came out as a squeak. I could feel myself beginning to wheeze.

"I told you so," declaimed an ominous voice. It was Ms. Robins.

The dog—or was it a wolf?—barked again. The blades descended...

My heart pounding, I sat up in bed, sick with relief. What a nightmare! The last time I'd had a bad dream like this was after I'd eaten two full pints of Ben & Jerry's Tubby Hubby ice cream before bed. This was worse. I wondered whether Riva had had a bad night too. The only one who I could guarantee had slept well was that *farshtunkener* hound Schultz, who was doubtlessly tired out by the unexpected midnight fun and games.

Although it was only 6:30 am, I figured I'd better work out a program of action with Riva as soon as possible, so by 7 am, I was at her door. I'd tiptoed past Josh, who of course, was asleep. I'd heard him come in after 2 am.

"Who is it?"

"Shoirlock. Who do you think it is?" I snapped. I was too tired and dispirited to even make an effort to be chirpy this morning. Come to think of it, I hadn't even bothered with a pre-breakfast snack. That shows how down I was.

Riva, in a flannel robe and slippers, opened the door.

She smiled when she saw my face. "Come on, Ellie. It isn't the end of the world. So we broke a lock and looked around Ms. Robins' office. What can they do to us? Kick us out? There are other retirement homes. They can send us to jail? Nu, we'd survive. Martha Stewart did. Anyway, they wouldn't do that. George was just trying to scare us."

"They could tell my son," I said gloomily. "Now that would be bad. You don't know Josh."

"Bad? You don't know from bad. Bad is when you are nine years old and your parents send you away to a strange country to escape the Nazis. And then you never see your mother or father again."

She was right. Nothing could even approach that. I was ashamed.

"Got anything to eat?" I asked.

Riva burst out laughing. "Now that's my Ellie. Here, try some mandelbrot."

"Not bad," I said, munching on the nutty cookie. "I can make better ones, but these are pretty good, for a bought cookie. So, what am I going to tell them? You've got your excuse—you couldn't sleep—but I have to think of a good story to justify my being in the office. That isn't going to be easy."

I paced around the small unit, thinking out loud. "The door was open and I was looking to see if anybody had broken in and had stolen anything? I was sleepwalking? The dog somehow opened the door? If he could lock Maurice in the freezer, I guess he could do that."

Riva pondered. "No, there is no way out of it. We will have to tell the truth. You and I were trying to discover who had killed Sam and Maurice and suspected Ms. Robins. We found her office door unlocked—no need to go into the credit card business—and decided to see if we could find evidence. They may very well decide that the Menorah needs no more bad publicity and hush it up."

"I don't see why you have to be involved," I said. "George seemed to believe you."

"Nevertheless, I was involved, and I will take responsibility," she said firmly. I felt a rush of affection for her. Riva may have been prickly, but she had integrity and she was turning out to be a true friend. She would share whatever the Menorah management had in store for us.

"Now let us hold our heads up high and go to breakfast," she said.

It wasn't easy to pretend nothing was wrong, as we ran the gauntlet of the *yentas* in the lobby, where Mollie, of course, was holding forth to a bunch of wide-eyed ladies. They all stopped talking when they saw us. So they had heard already. George must have opened his big mouth and the bush telegraph was operating even at 8 am. We could see Ms. Robins, in her office, talking to George, who was gesticulating. It was all too easy to imagine what they were talking about. I walked faster, in the hope that they wouldn't see me.

In the dining room, the buzz started as soon as we walked in. Bernice and Pearl were already waiting for us impatiently.

"Well!" said Pearl. "George is saying that you broke into Ms. Robins' office last night. I never figured you for a thief, Ellie," she said in her high-handed way. "Somebody must be a bad influence on you." She cast a sideways glance at Riva.

"Ellie is a thief?" Bernice picked up on that and looked at me wide-eyed. "Are you a murderer too? Did you kill Maurice and Sam? Did you have sex with Sam?"

"No," said Riva sharply. "Ellie is not a thief or a murderer. Please don't go around telling such lies."

Pearl raised an eyebrow. "She was in the kitchen when Maurice fell out of the freezer. And come to think of it, she was nearby when Sam died."

"I didn't kill anybody, Pearl. Why would I?" But I could see that all around the room, residents were staring at our table. I was clearly suspect number one.

Somehow, I had lost my appetite, which for me, was pretty unusual. I got up; no reason I should sit through this kind of third degree. Anyway, I had food in my suite. And I had something important to tell Riva; something that had slipped my mind before.

But before we could leave, we were stopped by Noah, who dashed over to us in the dining room. His jeans, hanging precariously low on his skinny behind, seemed to defy gravity. I couldn't imagine how they stayed up.

"Hey, Bubbie, I hear you robbed the office last night, and you didn't call me. That was totally not cool. I could have been the lookout." He seemed more impressed than angry though, and added, "How did you break in anyway?"

"In your dreams am I going to tell you," I said. "And I'm Mrs. Shapiro, not Bubbie."

"Pull up your jeans," said Riva sharply. "Everyone here can see your tush."

Noah grunted and yanked his jeans a few inches higher.

"Whatever."

Riva he listened to. Me, not so much. I wondered what you had to do to project so much authority. Not bake cookies, that was for sure.

"Come on," I said to the two of them. "We're not welcome here."

Once again, we ran the gauntlet of busybodies in the lobby, and headed for my living room, where I made a fresh pot of coffee and brought out the remains of the rugelach. Noah made quick work of them.

"So, what did you find in the files that was so important?" asked Riva.

"I'll tell you what I found out. Do you know what Ms. Robins' maiden name was? Klara Grobel."

They both looked at me. "So?"

"Klara Grobel! Don't you get it? She's German."

Riva shook her head slowly. "Ellie, World War II ended in 1945. Even if she's German, and even if this is a Jewish retirement home, nobody could possibly accuse her of being a Nazi. She was born long after the war."

"That's true," I said. "But then why did she change her name?"

"She only changed her first name. Her second name comes from her husband. Maybe she didn't like the name Klara. I don't blame her; it's old fashioned."

"What's a Nazi?" asked Noah.

Riva and I looked at each other. Where do you even begin? Noah was a trial, I had to say.

87

"Don't they teach you anything in school?" she asked. "Have you never heard of Hitler or the Kindertransport or the Holocaust?"

"Yeah, I heard of Hitler. I know he was a bad guy. He's a character in my 'Bionic Command' video game. You don't need to treat me like I'm dumb or something. Anyway, I know more than you two do about computers and lots of other things."

He had a point. I tried to calm the two of them down.

"Let's not get off track here. We have to find out who killed Sam and Maurice, not insult each other. I think the next step should be to follow Ms. Robins, and find out what we can about her. She's still a suspect."

"Yeah!" Noah was enthusiastic. Riva was less so. "Very well, although I am not sure that it will lead to anything. But before that, it might be a good idea to go back to the Community Archive and see if we can discover what she was looking up there. Now that we know she was German, there might be a link."

My heart sank at the thought of confronting Hal. He might have heard by now that I had gone snooping around, after promising him that I wouldn't. I had deliberately lied. How would that affect his opinion of me? Was this budding friendship, or whatever it was, over before it had even begun?

Meanwhile, Josh was taking a shower in the bathroom. With any luck, we could be out of the suite before he finished. Of course it turned out to be too much to hope for.

Rubbing his head with a towel, Josh, wearing my toweling robe and looking surprised, wandered into the living room. He did a double take when he saw the crowd.

"Hello! Who have we here?"

"This is my friend Riva, and this is Noah, Sam's grandson. He's been helping me with my computer skills," I said.

Noah held up his hand for a high-five. Josh grinned, slapped his palm and said, "Hi there, Noah. So how's my mom doing on the computer?"

Please Noah. Keep your mouth shut about what we've been up to, I thought. But it was obvious that Noah, being the idiot he was, was about to spill the beans.

Fortunately, I was saved by a loud knock on the door.

It was Lieutenant Johnson and Detective Smyth, looking a lot more annoyed than they had the last time our paths had crossed.

"It's you again," I said, stating the obvious.

"You were expecting maybe Ghostbusters?" said Lieutenant Johnson. "Of course it's us. If you're caught breaking and entering a private office, who do you expect to come calling?"

He scratched his head.

"For an old dame, you cause a lot of trouble. What on earth were you thinking? Do you need money? Did you think Ms. Robins kept money in her desk?"

"What's this all about?" asked Josh. "My mother was breaking and entering? Are you crazy?"

"No, I'm not crazy. I wish I could say the same thing for your mother. She's in trouble, along with her sidekick here."

"Mom, what's going on?" Josh sounded seriously worried.

I honestly couldn't think of a thing to say that would get me out of this mess.

"Well?"

Detective Smyth whispered to him, "She's probably a little s. e. n. i. l. e."

Josh looked angry. He could call me names, but nobody else could. Before he could interject, Riva had something to say.

"She's not senile and she's not deaf," said Riva. "What's more she can spell. Please do us the honor of treating us like the intelligent people we are."

She glanced at Noah and amended, "...that Ellie and I are. Let me explain. We told you before that we think Sam and Maurice were murdered. You foolishly ignored us. Possibly Ms. Robins is the culprit. We were looking for evidence."

Lieutenant Johnson guffawed. "And what evidence did you find for this ridiculous accusation?"

"None, "admitted Riva, in a dignified tone. "Yet."

"And you won't. Because there is none. Sam died of natural causes and Maurice had an accident. I'll let it pass this time, but I warn you, we're not going to take any more of your guff. If anything like this ever happens again, you'll be charged. By the way, how did you get in the office?" he asked curiously. "Ms. Robins swears she locked it."

"Yeah, that's what I want to know too," said Noah. I gave him a shove. Shut up, Noah.

"No, the door was open," said Riva.

"Hmm..." He looked at us skeptically. The two of us stared back, eyes innocently wide open.

"Stay out of trouble." That was his parting shot.

"Up yours," retorted Noah, giving Johnson's retreating back the finger. But that was after the door had closed.

❧ Chapter Sixteen ❧

Riva and I were relieved, but a little glum when the detectives left. Fortunately, we had escaped with nothing but a tongue-lashing from the cops and a worried look from Josh.

I had fed Josh a cock-and-bull story about getting locked in Ms. Robins' office by mistake, and although he didn't really buy it, he seemed to have reserved judgment. At least he wasn't dragging me out of the Menorah by the hair. Maybe he was beginning to think that Officer Smyth had a point when she claimed I was s. e. n. i. l. e.

On the other hand, we were still being treated with indulgence, as if we were biddies with wild imaginations, rather than sensible people who should be listened to. There was a murderer on the loose in the Menorah, and the police refused to believe it. Of course the residents believed it, but since they were old, no one believed them either. Josh might well believe it too, but he wasn't going to be able to stop me searching for the truth if I could help it, or so I sincerely hoped.

The police wanted us to stop investigating. 'Stay out of trouble' was the way they put it—but if we did, who would be killed next? No, we had to keep going.

The entrance lobby was crowded with people bidding farewell to Joyce Kramer, who was moving out. Her daughter dragged suitcases and the parrot cage to a waiting car, while Joyce hugged a bevy of sorrowful women.

"Good-bye! Take care."

And our resident super-hypochondriac was gone.

Mollie, of course, was in her element. Sitting in state on the sofa, she proclaimed, "I heard that Joyce is moving into the Mount Carmel Assisted Living Residence. She's afraid to live here, now that people are getting killed. Here, look at this,"

She handed me a colorful brochure. "Everybody found this in their mail boxes this morning."

It appeared that the owners of the Mount Carmel Retirement Residence, a competitor of the Menorah, were making hay while the sun shone, so to speak. They had evidently heard about the *tsores* at the Menorah, and were actively recruiting.

I glanced at the brochure and read,

"The Mt. Carmel Senior Residence, offers an elegant and safe community which promotes well-being in a home-like, well-protected environment. Respectful independence, supportive services, and Jewish traditions all with family and community involvement, along with supreme concern for security…"

Right, I got the idea.

Oy vey. What was Ms. Robins going to think about all this? And more important, what were her bosses going to think? She was in trouble. I looked around for her. Ms. Robins was in the lobby, but what had happened to our usually self-confident warden?

Pristine no more, her hair, normally styled into a sleek, lacquered helmet, was messy and oddly off kilter. She was wearing the usual business-like suit, but her blouse was buttoned unevenly and there was a run in her hose. Even more alarming, her usual air of authority seemed to have disappeared. She seemed frantic, in an unfocussed way and to my relief, ignored us as we left, even though we knew that George had told her that we had searched her office.

Schultz barked, keyed up by all the excitement, but it made no impression. Ms. Robins had totally lost it. I had to stop myself from feeling sorry for her and reminded myself that she could still be the murderer.

"I heard that the owners are coming to do an inspection," said Molly, the know-it-all. "Ms. Robins seems really nervous about that. With all the people leaving, and Maurice dead in the kitchen, she's scared that she may lose her job."

She glanced at Riva.

"You'd better watch out, Riva. People have been complaining about your dog, and I think the owners are planning to check Shultz out."

I remembered that Ms. Robins now knew about Riva's background as a *Kindertransport* child, and that neither she nor the owners would be likely to want to antagonize her.

"How can they check out Schultz?" I said. "For his pedigree? That's ridiculous."

"No, it's not ridiculous. You know how in co-op apartments, the committee checks out someone who wants to buy an apartment in the building. Well, I heard they check out pets too. That's what the owners are probably planning to do. They want to make sure he's well behaved."

"Schultz is a smart dog," I said. "He'll pass the test." I was lying in my teeth, of course.

But Riva looked concerned.

સ ✖

At the Community Archive, Hal was pacing around, steaming. Riva and I put on brave faces; Noah looked, for once, interested.

"Ellie, I told you that playing around with detecting could be dangerous. You promised me that you would stop."

"I didn't really promise," I said.

"You did!"

"Hey, I had my fingers crossed behind my back. Shoirlock doesn't give up that easy."

Hal rolled his eyes. "You're no Shoirlock; you're more like that klutzy Inspector Clouseau in *The Pink Panther*. What on earth were you thinking, breaking into Ms. Robins' office?"

"Ah, but I found out something," I said.

"Yeah, she found out something," added Noah, popping his gum.

"Remove that gum please," ordered Riva. "I don't want to see it again."

"You're a bunch of clowns, do you know that?" said Hal, with a heavy sigh. "Ok, I'll bite. What did you find out."

"Ms. Robins is German. Also, she has a child," I said.

"Well," said Hal, "so what?"

"That is what I said," said Riva. I glared at her. Whose side was she on?

"I'm not sure yet what it means, but she was hiding information, so it meant something. Maybe there's more that we don't know about, and Sam was blackmailing her. That would give her a motive to kill him."

Hal paused. "She was German? Then it's interesting that when she was last here in the Community Archive, she asked if we had a copy of the latest Yad Vashem Report on the Investigation and Prosecution of Nazi War Criminals. Yad Vashem is Israel's official memorial to the victims of the Holocaust and it publishes a lot of research material."

To Riva, that seemed important. "Why would she want to read such a publication? Does she suspect that someone in the Menorah was a war criminal in disguise, like that man, John Demjanjuk, who lived in the US but actually was once a guard at a Polish death camp?"

I couldn't imagine a former Nazi war criminal wanting to live in the Menorah, but who knew? Stranger things had happened. Well, maybe stranger things hadn't happened, but it did seem even more important that we follow Ms. Robins and see what she got up to. When I mentioned our plan, though, Hal hit the roof.

"What? You're going to follow her? That's nuts. Riva can hardly walk, anyway. And I'll bet you plan to take Noah and Schultz."

"Of course," said Riva.

"That dog gets you into even more trouble than you manage to get into yourselves, and taking a kid along is foolhardy."

"I can take care of these BOOFs," offered Noah.

"BOOFS?"

"Burnt out old farts," Noah explained. "Jeez, you're so out of touch."

"That's it. You can go back and help your parents clean up your grandfather's suite," said Riva firmly.

"No!" Noah said hastily." I didn't mean it. I just meant I'd keep an eye on you."

"You? You can't even keep your jeans up." Hal was dismissive. "The whole thing is ridiculous. I forbid it."

That made me angry. "You forbid it? What gives you the authority? I've spent my life listening to other people tell me what to do, and it took me more than 70 years to finally say no. If I want to bake cookies, I will. If I want to follow a murderer, I'll do that too. You don't need to come. We don't need you."

"Fine, you don't need me? So don't. I thought you had more sense."

He left the room. Well, that was that. So much for senior love. It had ended before it had even begun. I may have won the battle, but had I lost the war?

"True love is foiled," said Noah, playing an invisible violin in the air. Riva opened her mouth to say something, and, for once, thought better of it. I drew in a shaky breath.

"We leave after Ms. Robins does, tonight."

"We don't have a car," said Riva. "And how will we know when Ms. Robins is leaving? We can't all hang out in the lobby."

"We'll solve the transportation problem when we come to it," I replied, with more certainty than I felt. "If worse comes to worse, we'll call a taxi. And we'll ask Mollie to let us know when she's getting ready to leave. She can see into Ms. Robins' office from the sofa."

But we hadn't reckoned on Mollie's shrewdness.

"Why do you want to know when Ms. Robins is leaving?" she wanted to know, when I asked her if she'd tell me when Ms. Robins was showing signs of going home. "Do you want to break into her office again?"

"No, Mollie. I, uh..am trying to avoid her and I want to know when I can pass through the lobby without her seeing me."

Mollie bought that story.

"Am I part of your team now?" she asked. "Do I get a detective name?"

She looked thrilled. How on earth had she ever figured out that we had a team? But now that I thought about it, she would be a good addition. In fact, we may have made a mistake not including her from the beginning. As a spy and an informer, not to mention a lookout, Mollie was without peer. She knew everything.

"Sure, Mollie. You can be Nancy Drew. Or Jane Bond. Here," I jerked Noah's cell phone out of his hand, and gave it to her.

"Hey!" he shouted. "Give that back."

"You'll get it back when Mollie calls us. This is what you do. When Ms. Robins leaves, you press this, then this, then press where it says my name. When it rings and I answer, you give us a code word. The code word is 'mazal tov'. Do you think you can remember that?

'Mazal tov. Sure, I got it."

"And you don't tell anyone. Not anyone! Understand?" said Riva.

Mollie got up and shuffled towards the elevator, moving amazingly quickly for a woman of 93. "I have to get ready," she said. "I have to dress in character."

Oh brother. I couldn't imagine which character would be more startling—Mollie dressed as an 18 year old girl sleuth or Mollie as 007, shaken, not stirred. Dear God, I hoped she didn't have a gun.

Riva, Noah, Schultz and I spent the rest of the day in my suite, with no sign of Hal. I filled the time by baking nothings, a kind of airy biscuit with lots of eggs that my mother had taught me to make. Riva read and Schultz got underfoot. Noah fidgeted. Eventually, at around 5:30 pm, the telephone rang. Nuts. We would miss supper.

"Mazal tov! Mazal tov!" Mollie shouted.

No doubt everyone around her would be puzzled as to why Mollie was issuing congratulations over a cell phone for no reason, but I wasn't going to worry about that. Now Mollie stage whispered, "She looks like she's getting ready to leave! She's packing her briefcase. Hurry!"

We hurried. In the lobby, I stopped dead when I saw her. Mollie had opted for a bizarre interpretation of Nancy Drew, the fictional girl detective. She was wearing a beret and had arranged what we could see of her sparse burgundy-tinted hair in a 1950's bob style. Her skirt was full and belted—obviously adapted from a muu-muu—and she wore a sweater that fell sadly slack over her scrawny chest. To complement the look, Mollie had chosen "Fire and Ice" red lipstick which had to date back to the 1950s, sky blue eye shadow and false eyelashes heavily dotted with mascara.

"I found an old Nancy Drew book in the library," she said. "I copied the picture on the cover. Do you like it?"

Noah burst out laughing. Riva shook her head. I gave her a look:

why rain on Mollie's parade? Never mind that Nancy's boyfriend, Ned Nickerson would have had a heart attack, had he ever existed in real life.

But now we were faced with a dilemma. None of us had a car, and Ms. Robins was already turning off the lights in her office. We didn't have much time. Fortunately, her telephone rang. That would give us a little more leeway. I craned my neck to see outside. The Menorah van was parked in the driveway, with George, the security guy who doubled as the driver whenever he was needed, smoking a cigarette not far away. He might well have left the keys in the van.

I looked at the van meaningfully.

"Don't even think about it," said Riva. "Really, Ellie. You have as about as much sense as Noah."

Sometimes she really got my goat, although, I had to admit, this was not one of those times. Hijacking the van would be a pretty dumb idea. Riva was right. But what then?

"I can take my dad's car," said Noah. "I know how to drive."

"Forget it," I said. "You don't have a license." Noah looked as if that were but an irrelevant detail.

"You are not going to like this idea, but I think we should try to convince Hal to drive us," said Riva.

"No!"

"Yeah," said Mollie, shaking drops from the thick mascara caked on her eyelashes and leering. "That guy is a looker."

Naturally, Riva ignored me. "I will call him." She took Noah's phone from Mollie

"What is the number of the Community Archive, Ellie?"

How did she know that I had memorized it? How embarrassing. I muttered the number.

"Hal? This is Riva. We have considered what you said about following Ms. Robins, and we have thought of a solution. You will come with us and look after us. And if you do that, we will allow you to decide what we do and what we don't do. Then you can be certain that we don't get into trouble."

There was a long pause. I couldn't imagine what Hal was saying.

"Right now," Riva answered him. "Ms. Robins is getting ready to leave her office, and we are outside."

Another pause.

"Very well. We agree."

"What did we agree to?" I asked warily.

"We agreed that he would drive, but that we wouldn't do anything dangerous, and he would be the one to decide what was dangerous. We are not in a position to make a better deal. I have the feeling that he is a little sorry that he was so overbearing and that he wants to make up with you, Ellie."

"Hmm," I said, but I felt my spirits lighten. Noah, that irritating kid, played his imaginary violin in the air again. Mollie looked interested. No doubt the residents would be regaled tomorrow with the story of this romance, which she would probably inflate to a full-blown affair. I could just imagine what Bernice would have to say—"Are you having sex with Hal, Ellie?" The very idea made my heart pound..

Fortunately, Ms. Robins' telephone call seemed to be taking a lot of time, and Hal pulled up in his car before she appeared. He did a double take when he saw Mollie in her Nancy Drew get-up.

"You're coming too? Along with Ellie, Riva and the dog?"

"You betcha. I'm the lookout. I'm riding shotgun. I'll have you know I'm an important part of this team. Where's your motor scooter? I want to sit on the back of it."

Hal gave a sigh. "Well, I suppose it could have been worse. It could have been Bernice and we would have had to stop at the restroom in every gas station on the way. Stay away from the motor scooter, Mollie. We're driving in the car, not the scooter. Stop kvetching. Get in, girls, and fast. Here comes Ms. Robins."

With Schultz hanging out of the window and Mollie banging her cane against the seat in front in excitement, we followed her. We were off!

❧ Chapter Seventeen ❦

I have no idea what you expect to discover from this adventure," grumbled Hal. I didn't reply, because I didn't really know either.

It would be pretty embarrassing to follow Ms. Robins, only to end up waiting for her outside a supermarket and then trailing her home. This adventure was more in the nature of doing something, no matter how ineffectual. My incorrigible curiosity, also, had its effect. Ms. Robins may or may not have been blackmailed, or a murderer, but what was behind her glossy mask? No one knew.

"Call me nosy but I really, really want to know more about Ms. Robins," I said.

"Ok, I'll call you nosy. You're nosy," said Noah, predictably. Pleased at his joke, he hooted with laughter like a hyena. Hal smiled, darn him.

It was a sleety, frosty night, with no stars visible. Were we nuts going out into the Minnesota winter in mid-January for no good reason, when we could just as easily be curled up at home with hot chocolate? I was having second thoughts. Hal had hacked the ice off the front windshield, but with the window open for Schultz, it was so cold that we could see our breath in white puffs. I shivered in my down parka.

"Can you keep the dog's head inside the car? If Ms. Robins looks in her rear-view mirror, she'll recognize him," I said. It was hopeless, though. Schultz was enjoying himself and couldn't be dragged away from the window. If Ms. Robins looked in the rear view mirror, it was just too bad for us.

Ms. Robins headed to the outskirts of Aurora and kept going. We passed strip malls, bars, and used car lots. Could she really live in this part of the world? Surely she must be paid enough to live somewhere better.

Now we were in the country. It was snowing harder. There seemed to be nothing around but flat, white country, with a grain elevator in the distance.

"Stop at a gas station," ordered Mollie.

"Mollie, surely you don't have to go the rest room. You sound like Bernice," I said.

"I just want to put some more lipstick on. I think I've licked it all off,"

"We're not stopping," said Riva. She looked around. "Anyway, there are no gas stations. Where on earth are we?"

"There's a small town up ahead," said Hal. "Ms. Robins seems to be headed there."

He was right. At the outskirts of the town, which a signpost announced as Brandon, Ms. Robins stopped at a complex of small apartments. We pulled up a short distance behind her. She got out of her car, but instead of walking into the building, strode over to us and looked in disbelief from Hal, to me, to Riva, to Mollie, to Noah and to the dog. Admittedly, we were a rather odd crew. Mollie waved cheerfully.

"All right. What's this all about? Why have you been following me?"

"Uh..." No one could think of anything to say—except for Mollie, unfortunately.

"We're detectives," she chirped. "We think Sam was blackmailing you and you killed him."

Oh my God. This was beyond embarrassing, perhaps most of all for Hal, who considered himself the responsible adult of the group. He turned a deep red, but said nothing, which I could understand. What could he say?

Ms. Robins laughed. She roared—a hysterical belly laugh that went on and on, until I was alarmed. This wasn't what I had expected, but I was pleased she was taking it so well, if you could call this crazy reaction well.

Finally, she wiped her eyes. "I suppose you think this is my hideout. You're a bunch of idiots, but since you're here, come in. See for yourself what a murderer I am."

She chivvied us up the path, through the blowing snow, and unlocked the door of a ground floor apartment. A young man whooped with joy when he saw her.

"This is my son Jamie," she said, giving him a hug. He hugged her in return.

Jamie was about 19, with the slanted eyes and flat facial features that indicated Down Syndrome. He was good-looking, with dark hair and blue eyes, but he avoided eye contact with us and seemed uneasy and anxious when we entered, until he spied Schultz. Then he crouched down to hug the dog, who reciprocated with licks.

We followed Ms. Robins into the kitchen, where a woman was helping another young man fry omelets. Two other young people were chatting while they set a table. They looked up with interest as we came in. The kitchen was simple but adequate, with a well-worn wooden table and chairs and a full complement of appliances. On a bulletin board, I could see three daily schedules, birthday cards and various drawings. There was a vase of flowers in the center of the table and hip-hop music blared from a radio.

Ms. Robins introduced us. "Meet Mary, Tom and Sam and Mrs. Jeffries. As you can see, this is a supervised group home for young adults. Jamie has learned to manage for himself quite well," she said, putting an arm affectionately around her son, who had now picked up Schultz and was cuddling him. "He has a part-time job at a car wash and he gets there himself on public transport. I'm very proud of him."

We could see that she was.

"Now you can understand why my job at the Menorah is so important to me. It takes a huge part of my salary, but keeping Jamie here means everything to me. He's all I've got and I'm all he's got. My ex-husband left us when Jamie was three.

"Do you know how hard it is to keep it all together? My hair— it's a wig."

She tore the wig off, and I gasped. Her hair was short and straight, brown shot through with grey. She looked 10 years older, but oddly, more attractive. Now that she was no longer trying to be authoritarian, she seemed much more human. I actually felt sorry for her.

"You think I killed Sam?" She laughed. "I wanted to kill him. The day he died was one of the happiest days of my life. But I didn't murder him."

"Why did you want him dead?" said Hal, who had found his tongue. That was what we all wanted to know, of course.

"Mollie is right; he was blackmailing me," she said simply. "It was because of what he saw me reading in the Community Archive.

I gasped. "That you're German?"

"No. That my father was a Nazi. He managed to hide his background and get visas for us to enter the US a few years after the war."

"I see, said Hal slowly. "I remember now. You were reading the 'Report on the Investigation and Prosecution of Nazi War Criminals.' It lists Nazi criminals who were never convicted. I suppose you found your father listed. But how did Sam connect that to you?"

Her eyes darkened. Moving deliberately, she put the kettle on and took cups out of the cupboard.

"Sam was very chatty," she said. "He told me he was interested in genealogy and he asked me about my own name. I told him that Robins was my husband's name, but my maiden name had been Grobel. I never dreamed he'd follow up on it. He must have done some research on his computer. A few days later, he stopped by my office, and told me that if I didn't pay him $500, he would let the owners know that my father was a Nazi."

There was a collective intake of breath. Well, yes, that would do it. If the residents of the Menorah found out that their administrator was the daughter of a Nazi, they would want her kicked out for sure.

"Is your father still alive?" I asked.

"No. He died years ago, but that wouldn't make much difference to the residents of the Menorah," she said.

She was right. There was nothing more to say, and after shaking hands with Jamie and apologizing to Ms. Robins, we left. On the way home, Mollie looked dazed. In all her experience of retailing gossip, she had never had a scoop like this one. I supposed it was hopeless to expect her to keep quiet, but I tried.

"Mollie, you have to keep this secret. Ms. Robins will be fired if people know about her Nazi father, and she won't be able to support her son."

"Not only that," added Hal. "If Sam were blackmailing Ms Robins, he might very well be blackmailing others too, including the person who murdered him and very possibly he was blackmailing Maurice too. That person is desperate not to be found out. He's dangerous. If he murdered two people, he might very well murder again. And we might be on the list."

Mollie nodded, but I wasn't reassured. Gossip was her passion; I would even say her addiction.

I was even less confident of her discretion when back at the Menorah, Mollie promptly sat down on her sofa in the entrance, no doubt waiting for her fellow *yentas* to arrive. They had probably been waiting for her, because she was immediately joined by a bevy of other residents, who had taken note of Mollie's odd get-up, and wanted to hear the whole story.

Molly was irrepressible and in her glory. Nothing was going to stop her. She didn't have bad intentions, but in order to spread her story, she would convince herself that Ms. Robins wouldn't be fired.

Somberly, we parted in the lobby. I had no doubt about it—it was time to bake something. Maybe the soothing action of rolling dough would give me some idea of where we could go from here. Riva followed me, with Schultz.

"What are you going to bake now?" she asked.

I smiled. "How did you know I was going to bake something?"

"Well, what else would you do, except eat?"

She was right, sort of. I would do both. I would bake, but first I would eat. I decided to stop by the kitchen to see what was going on, and what supplies I could pilfer.

So here I was in the kitchen again. The last time I'd been here, a corpse had tumbled out of the freezer onto me. The time before, I'd made blintzes for a *shiva*. I shivered. Maybe it had been a mistake coming in again. There were, as they say, bad vibes here.

But, on the other hand, Tommy was glad to see me and that warmed my heart.

"Ellie! I missed you. Have you come to help out?"

"Not this time. I just felt like cooking something and thought I'd find some inspiration here. What's for lunch tomorrow?"

"Got any ideas? What about that potato pie thing you make? Can you show me how you do it?"

"Potato kugel? Sure, I can do that."

I got out some potatoes and began to grate them. I was in no real hurry to return to my suite. I could help Tommy. When the potatoes were grated, I mixed them with eggs, matzo meal, seasonings and oil.

"You bake the mixture until the top is brown and the inside soft," I instructed, as I mixed. "I guarantee it'll be a hit. You can multiply the recipe to make enough for everyone."

As we worked at the stainless steel counter, Tommy asked, "So tell me, what's the gossip? I hear that you and the guy in the Community Archive are an item? True?"

"Sadly, no," I admitted. "So far, it's going nowhere. He's bossy and I'm stubborn. It's not a very promising combination."

"Hey, you deserve the best," he said. "Give it time. If it's meant to be, it will be."

"At my age, time is what I haven't got," I said glumly. "If it's meant to be, it better be soon or it won't be at all."

He patted my shoulder. "I have a good feeling about this. Trust me. It's gonna happen."

I smiled. Tommy was trying to cheer me up, and I appreciated it. But now that I was here, maybe I could find out something about the murders, if there was anything to find out.

"Tommy," I said carefully, "do you have any idea at all who could have trapped Maurice in the freezer? Did Maurice know something about who killed Sam? Maybe someone wanted to stop Maurice from telling what he knew."

"Yeah, I've thought about that. Maurice told you that he had a scam going with the food bills. I knew about it and I wasn't happy, but I kept my mouth shut. I have a feeling that Sam may have found out. I came into the kitchen once and found them arguing. Maurice was worried, no doubt about that. You saw for yourself."

"Sam was a blackmailer for sure, but who would have killed him or Maurice? Do you have any idea?"

I thought to myself that it would have been easy enough for Maurice to slip a few pills into Sam's plate.

Tommy shook his head. "Maurice was keen on money, but he was a small time fiddler. He wasn't making tons of money out of fiddling fruit and vegetable bills. It was more like a game to him.

I'm sure he would never resort to murder."

I had to agree.

"So," I said again, "if it wasn't Maurice who killed Sam, who did? And who killed Maurice?"

Tommy shook his head again. "Are you sure it wasn't Ms. Robins?"

"No, I'm not absolutely sure," I said, "but my feeling is that she's innocent. It's true that she had motive and opportunity, but still, I believe her."

I remembered how she had ripped off her wig, as though she were done hiding. That had the ring of truth. I also remembered how she had hugged her son. She would never do anything to put him in danger. If she had murdered Sam and been caught, what would happen to Jamie?

It was all too much. I popped the kugel batter in the fridge, helping myself to some tasty looking brownies at the same time, and decided it was time to think things over. Enough adventure for one day!

✤ Chapter Eighteen ✥

I'm missing lunch," I grumbled. First we had missed supper because we were trailing Ms Robins, and now we were missing lunch. This was too much. I hope the cops eventually appreciated the sacrifices I was making in the interest of finding a killer.

The strategy meeting was being held at lunchtime on purpose, so that everyone else would be in the dining room and we wouldn't be seen together. No one would miss us, because they were all buzzing about the inspection visit by the owners of the Menorah, which, according to gossip, was due to take place any day. I hadn't really been pleased about Mollie inviting herself along, but she had stuck to us like glue. She wasn't going to miss a thing.

"Have a cookie," offered Hal.

"That isn't lunch," I said, but I took one anyway. Schultz, who was the only one except myself who seemed to resent missing a meal, licked my hand and I passed him a cookie.

"Stop complaining, Ellie," snapped Riva. "We are here to discuss our future moves. There is a killer in the Menorah, and we must find him, or her.

"Yes!" said Mollie eagerly. "We're detectives. We have to detect."

"So let's sum up," said Hal. "Sam was killed, maybe, by an overdose of pills which reacted with alcohol. The question is, who had a motive and who had opportunity? We know that Ms.

Robins had a motive—she was being blackmailed—and she also had opportunity, since she was in and out of the kitchen. On the other hand, it doesn't make sense that she would do anything that might threaten her son's security and being found out as a murderer would certainly do that."

"I just have a feeling that she didn't do it," I said. "The way she acted yesterday seemed sincere to me."

"You are too sentimental, Ellie." Riva was her usual acerbic self. "Feelings are not proof. We will have to leave her on the suspect list. Who else had a motive?"

She picked up a pen and began writing.

"Anybody else Sam was blackmailing. It might have been someone that he found on JLove, who would have been humiliated at being found out. Someone like Bernice, for example."

"I'll ask around," suggested Mollie. "Maybe it was Bernice."

"NO!" we all shouted together. "You won't ask around, Mollie. This is meant to be a secret between us."

Mollie's face fell. What fun was it going to be being Nancy Drewski if she couldn't tell everyone all about it?

"Bernice?" Hal snorted. "You've suggested that before, but I think you should drop that idea. She can't even find her way to the bathroom alone."

That gave me an idea. "Ah, but why is she going to the bathroom so often? On television shows, when someone goes the bathroom, it's because they want to snort cocoa."

"Cocaine, not cocoa," said Hal. He shook his head and started laughing. "I can't think of anyone less likely than Bernice to be a drug addict!"

"She has a weak bladder, not a cocaine habit," said Riva. "I know that, because we were both in the nurse's waiting room together a few weeks ago and she told me that was a problem."

"She told me that too," added Mollie. Well, that was the final word on the subject. If Mollie knew that particular piece of news, it was likely to be true.

But going to the bathroom gave her an opportunity to go wherever she wanted to without anybody being suspicious. I was getting excited. "Remember just before Sam died? Bernice stumbled into his table as she was wandering around. She could easily have popped a few pills into his knish."

Hal was dubious. "I really have a hard time seeing Bernice as a killer, but I'll give your idea the benefit of the doubt. She's suspect number two. Write it down, Riva. OK—here's another possibility. What about Joyce, the hypochondriac? She figures she's dying anyway, so she might as well get rid of Sam, who is driving her crazy with his tricks."

"Murder is not something to make a joke about," said Riva, but I couldn't help laughing. In my view, either you laughed or you cried at what life throws at you and you might as well enjoy yourself.

"You guys are so lame," put in Noah, "except for the cocaine angle." He waved his hands around so wildly that he knocked his cap off, revealing spikes that were bottle blond today.

"Yeah, I like that. I bet someone from outside was dealing coke to all the old geezers here. Maybe the postman or the van driver. My Zaidie got wise and someone put an overdose in his knish. Then he tried to store the rest in the freezer, and Maurice caught him and the dealer locked him in the freezer. It all makes sense. I bet the police will agree with me."

"It makes no sense at all," said Hal, who started laughing again. "There are so many holes in that story that I don't know where to begin. You must have got the plot from a computer game."

"Yeah, I did. There's this game, Murder 2, where…"

"This is not a computer game and you are not to involve the police!" Riva interrupted.

"Chill,Bubbie,"…he muttered under his breath "Whatever."

"So what's the plan?" Silence. Hal and Riva were stumped. Riva looked at her list, and slowly crumpled it up.

We needed to know if Sam had blackmailed anyone else. But how?

I thought of something. If you wanted to know anything around the Menorah, rely on gossip. So Mollie hadn't come up with the goods. What was the next best source of information? Of course—the Menorah mahjong players. They met Mondays after lunch, in the Vintage Cafe, where eight or nine bridge tables were set up to accommodate a few dozen players. And those players just loved to gossip.

"Can any of you play mahjong?" I asked.

Riva turned up her nose. (I might have guessed; mahjong was

too low-class for her. Bridge or chess, maybe. Mahjong was for peasants.)

Hal: "Nope."

Mollie: "I like to talk to people, not play games with them."

Noah: "Is it a computer game?"

Schultz wagged his tail. He was willing. (Sorry Schultz.)

So that left me. I could play mahjong, although I didn't very often.

Mahjong is a game that originates in China, but has become beloved, for some reason, by Jewish matrons. It's a little like rummy, except with rectangular tiles rather than playing cards. The tiles bear various symbols called bams, dots, cracks, winds, seasons and flowers. The idea is to draw and discard tiles in a certain order until one player is able to form a combination of tiles corresponding to one listed on a card put out by the National Mahjong League. This organization is the arbiter of all the rules of the game. You might call it the mahjong police.

To add a little excitement, the game is played for money, although not for very much. A big winner might take home the grand sum of $2 in an afternoon.

Can a game this innocent be cut-throat? You bet. Keen players did everything they could to win, including calling out other players for real or imagined infractions, and sometimes, even cheating. There were women at the Menorah who didn't speak to each other because of a quarrel over mahjong.

On Monday, I turned up at the Vintage Café with my mahjong card. The Vintage Café had an oak bar along one wall where coffee, tea and soft drinks were dispensed, and a sprinkling of decorative antiques—old tea cups, lace, and daguerreotypes—arranged on shelves, to underline the vintage theme. (Of course the real vintage objects were us.) By contrast, a professional modern Gaggia espresso machine hissed on the counter. I helped myself to a cup of cappuccino and looked around for a table at which I could play.

It was easy to find a table with a player missing, since often enough, a regular player was ill or otherwise occupied. Unfortunately, today that vacant spot was at a table with two cut-throat players, Sadie Diamond and Norma Vogel. Bernice made the fourth. Why she insisted on playing was beyond me, since it was all a little too complicated for her and someone usually had to help her out. Naturally, she was a regular loser, but she was good-natured about paying up.

Now how was I going to get them to dish the dirt on Sam without becoming suspicious?

"Did you know that in China, mahjong is considered a men's game?" I said innocently. That was my first gambit, as I sorted my hand.

"I wonder why men don't play here?" I added. "They might be good at it. Sam, for instance, had a good head for cards."

I was pleased with myself for thinking up that opening. Oh, I was crafty!

Sadie picked up on it. "Don't be silly, Ellie. The men here like poker or gin rummy, not mahjong. Sam was too much of a joker to take mahjong seriously. He would probably try to juggle the tiles instead of play with them."

Norma laughed. "He'd be a sore loser for sure."

"Why do you say that?" I asked. "He seemed like a nice guy."

"No, he wasn't," said Norma, picking up a tile and discarding another one. "Dolly Klein told me that he seemed real interested in her. He even asked her out to dinner. She was so excited, even though it turned out he only took her for the early bird special at the Pizzeria. Then he kept asking her questions about how rich her husband had been, and when the bill came, he said he left his wallet at home."

"Was she very angry?"

"I think she wasn't really angry, but she was a little humiliated. She made me promise not to tell anyone."

So much for that promise, I thought. A good piece of gossip always trumped a secret.

Could Dolly have killed Sam? I would have to talk to her, even though I didn't know her very well. But if Sam had tried it out on one woman, he might have done the same to others. There were plenty of rich ladies living at the Menorah. Come to think of it, given the prices the Menorah charged, there were few residents who weren't comfortably off.

"Was Sam interested in Pearl? She was rich," I asked Norma.

"Nah," she replied. "Sam knew better than to try anything with Pearl. She's such a snob. It's obvious she thinks that she's way too good for him. Like, she talks all the time about the wonderful marriages her daughters made."

"Right, to Jewish doctors," interjected Sadie "And her granddaughter is going to marry a fancy Jewish lawyer. No, she would never have looked at Sam."

I remembered the distain Pearl had shown when Sam started juggling knishes in the dining room, and I had to agree. She thought too highly of herself to be a target for Sam. And what would he ever blackmail her about? It was hard to imagine anyone less likely to do anything daring than Pearl.

Bernice interrupted, "Mahjong!" she shouted, waving her card in the air. That meant that she had completed one of the combinations on the card and had won that hand.

Norma was suspicious. Bernice rarely won. "Let's see your tiles," she said.

Bernice displayed her tile rack.

"You nut," said Sadie. "That's a flower, not a bam. You didn't win."

Bernice's eyes filled with tears. "I am not a nut."

"No, of course you aren't," I reassured her, glaring at Sadie. "Everyone makes mistakes."

Norma said, "You aren't perfect yourself, Sadie. I remember very well that you peeked at my tile rack last week, so that you would win."

"What a liar you are! I won because I'm a better player!"

The two women rose in their chairs. "I'm not going to play with you anymore, you cheater," announced Norma.

The others in the room were agog. No one was even pretending to play now. They were all listening intently, eyes sparkling and mouths open.

"You called me a liar. You're the liar."

"*Alte maksheyfe!*"

"Who are you calling an old witch? *Shtik drek!*"

"A piece of dung? Excuse me?"

Sadie picked up a tile and threw it at Norma. It hit her glasses, cracking a lens.

"I'm calling the police. You assaulted me!"

She threw a tile back. I ducked. It struck a woman sitting at a table opposite, who shrieked, "Did you see what Norma just did?

She hit me!"

She threw a tile back at Norma, but her aim was wild. It landed in a coffee cup with a splash.

By now, others had joined the fray. Tiles flew around the room. One hit Norma in the mouth and knocked her upper plate askew. Bernice laughed and pointed, and Norma slapped her.

It was chaos, but to tell the truth, I suspected that a good time was being had by all. It was probably 60 years since any of the mahjong girls had enjoyed a good fight, and they were having fun. But of course, it wouldn't do to admit that.

Norma adjusted her teeth, pulled out her cell phone and dialed 101.

"I'm being assaulted!" she screamed. "At the Menorah Retirement home." She hung up.

"What's going on here?" Ms. Robins—no surprise—had heard the racket and dashed into the room, followed by a parade of residents with wheelchairs, walkers or their own legs. Ms. Robins, no longer the nice person she had promised to become, was furious. I couldn't blame her. Actually, I almost preferred her this way. The new, sweet Ms. Robins was unnervingly unnatural.

"Sadie tried to kill me! She broke my glasses with a mahjong tile," whined Norma.

Sadie was now very red in the face. I was afraid that she might have a fit, and I tried to support her. "Get her some water, Bernice," I said, but that was expecting too much from Bernice, who was still sitting at the table, staring at the action. For once, she had forgotten the washroom.

A siren wailing in the distance became louder. I heard a car door slam, and then two police officers burst into the room.

Just my luck—of course it would have to be the team of Johnson and Smyth.

Lieutenant Johnson stopped dead when he saw me. "You! Didn't I tell you to stay out of trouble? Who did you assault?"

"I didn't assault anybody," I said with all the dignity I could muster. It didn't seem to make an impression.

"You always seem to be the center of some kind of chaos," said Officer Smyth. She looked around. The room had quietened down. Norma was showing off her broken glass lens to a gawking audience and staring daggers at Sadie, who had her own claque of women around her.

"Why is it that there's trouble wherever you are? They should expel you."

"This isn't reform school. I can't be expelled," I said huffily. "If you accuse me unjustly, you can be sued for false arrest, or libel or defamation or... or something else bad."

Lieutenant Johnson snorted. "I told you that you watch too much TV."

Ms. Robins intervened. "It had nothing to do with Ellie," she said. "Leave her alone. In fact, leave them all alone. The excitement is over. No one was hurt. It was just a little tiff over a game." She shooed them out of the room, and Johnson and Smyth left meekly enough. Even the cops were no match for Ms. Robins at her most overbearing.

Ms. Robins defending me? Maybe she had changed after all. Or maybe I had changed. Stick up for yourself, I had learned, and people respect you. Too bad it had taken over half a century to learn that lesson.

Slowly, the room emptied, leaving a mess of upturned tables and chairs, scattered tiles and broken glass. Nobody was left, except Bernice, who was sitting by herself at the table, in spite of the fact that the other three chairs had fallen on their sides. Her playing rack was still intact, all thirteen tiles neatly ordered. Tears were running down her cheeks.

"Mahjong," she said sadly, showing me her card. "I won."

❧ Chapter Nineteen ◈

I hugged poor Bernice, who was devastated by the fact that chaos had broken loose the one time in years she had managed to win at mahjong, or so she thought.

"Never mind. You'll win next time," I told her. Either that or she would have forgotten by the next time she played. That's of course assuming there would be a next time, given the riot and its consequences.

But something seemed to be happening out in the lobby. Could there possibly be more excitement at the Menorah today?

There was.

"The inspection team is here!" Mollie hobbled into the room in great excitement. "They're paying a surprise visit and they ran into the police."

What would the inspectors think of what was going on at the Menorah? And what would they make of the police inspecting a supposed assault? I didn't envy Ms. Robins having to deal with this. But of course, I wasn't going to miss the fun.

"Come on," I said to Riva, who had come in too, and followed me, trailing Schultz.

"You are far too nosy, Ellie," she told me, yet again. "This is not our business. Let's go to our suites."

Give it a rest, Riva, I thought to myself. I pretended I hadn't heard her and headed for the door, colliding with the inspectors, who had spied the damage in the Vintage Café from the lobby and were now heading in for a look around. Noah had appeared too.

"Holy shit," he said, when he saw the chaos.

I saw the Vintage cafe through their eyes: a woman—Bernice—sitting alone and crying, amid tables and chairs in disarray, broken coffee cups and mahjong tiles higgledy-piggledy on the floor. It looked more like the scene of the aftermath of a hurricane than a decorous coffee shop and lounge for elderly mahjong players.

The inspectors, trailed by an alarmed Ms. Robins, gaped at the scene. They didn't seem amused.

"Who are you?" an inspector asked me, rather rudely, I thought. Who did he think I was, the Easter bunny? Obviously, I was a resident. And why didn't he have the good manners to introduce himself?

"This is Mrs. Shapiro," Ms. Robins said, taking command. "She's been living here for a year. And this is Mrs. Mannheim, and her dog Schultz, and Noah, who is the grandson of a resident who passed away last week. Noah is just leaving," she said pointedly. He ignored her. There wasn't much she could do to get rid of him, short of hit him with a chair, or maybe a mahjong tile, so she continued.

"Mr. Owen represents Highridge Holdings and is paying us a visit, with Mr. Zarkis and Ms Gold, our geriatric psychologist."

I knew that although the Witbergs had donated money to build the Menorah Residence, Highridge Holdings was the company that actually ran it, as well as running about a dozen other retirement homes around the country. The firm provided top-rate services, in return for top dollar. Their brief was not a charitable one; Highridge Holdings was a business out to make a profit. If something went wrong at the Menorah, then adjustments would have to be made. I had no doubt that Ms. Robins was well aware of that fact.

She obviously wanted me to leave, but I thought I would stick around anyway. If I could help her, then I would, whether she liked it or not. Also, I might find out something interesting. They didn't call me nosy for nothing.

Mr. Owen ignored Riva and me. Young, good-looking and wafting a men's scent that was definitely not Old Spice, he had impeccably cut hair, an expensive-looking suit, Italian leather shoes and a look of distaste, as if he wondered what he was doing here with all these unattractive geriatrics. I guess he thought *he* was never going to grow old like us and have to live in a retirement residence. Ha! Just wait.

Mr. Zarkis, who was trailing Mr. Owen, was a rumpled looking middle-aged man, glasses askew, scribbling in a notebook. He wasn't making eye contact with anyone. I assumed he was the money man. He certainly looked like an accountant.

The third member of the party was unexpected; she was a woman who didn't look anything like a businesswoman. On the contrary, she had unruly curly hair, and wore a long denim skirt with an oversize sweater, giving her the appearance of a campus hippy, vintage 1970. My guess was that her task was to check up on the living conditions and satisfaction of the residents. If so, she would have her hands full today.

Unlike the other two inspectors, Ms Gold appeared very interested in the residents. She even patted Schultz. Enjoying the attention, the dog began running around wildly in circles, tongue hanging out, knocking over any chairs that were still left standing. He collided with Mr. Owen, who shuddered and ostentatiously wiped his trouser leg where Schultz had bumped into it, leaving a trail of drool.

Lips pursed, he said, "Pets are allowed in the Menorah residence, Ms Robins, but well-behaved animals, not undisciplined mutts. Why is this wild creature allowed to run around? After we finish our inspection, we will assess this dog's suitability to live here."

Poor Schultz! Test day had come for him. What a pain in the rear this Owen fellow was. Still, I couldn't help grinning—he had angered Riva and I wouldn't give much for his chances in a battle with her. He was in for it.

Before Ms. Robins could answer, Riva, in an icy voice, eyebrow raised and eyes narrowed, rose to her full 5 foot height and said, in her best schoolmarm manner, "Young man, who are you to tell me my dog is not disciplined enough to live here? He has better manners than you do. I pay for his board and the charge is not low. I will not put up with this."

"She's right," Mr. Zarkis, who had been looking at his notes, whispered. "She pays a sizable monthly fee for the dog."

Mr. Owen hastily backtracked. "Of course, Mrs.. uh ("Mannheim" interjected Riva.)... Mrs. Mannheim. We're not saying you can't keep your dog, just that he has to behave and will have to be assessed for suitability. I'm sure he will do just fine. In fact, we will give him his examination right now."

To illustrate his benevolence, he reached down with a barely concealed grimace to pat Schultz. "Good dog," he said.

Schultz, no fool, bared his teeth and growled. Mr. Owen backed away. He looked at Mr. Zarkis. "You give him the test."

"Uh, uh. I'm a cat man."

Schultz seemed to understand that, and growled again.

"You administer the dog test, Ms. Gold."

As low woman on the Highridge Holdings totem pole, Ms. Gold knew an order when she heard it. She didn't seem to have a choice, even though it was obvious she didn't have a clue in the world how to test a dog for fitness to live in a retirement home. But she was nothing if not willing and as a psychologist, she had assessment tools at her fingertips. Maybe not the most appropriate tools under the circumstances, but tools nevertheless.

"All *right*, Schultz," she began. "How are you feeling today?"

"He is feeling very well," said Riva. "He always feels well. It is foolish to ask him that question; he can't answer."

Schultz, feeling everyone's eyes on him, decided to perform his party trick. He stood on his hind legs, wobbled backwards, wagging his tail madly, and barked. Riva looked proud. Mr. Owen, Mr. Zarkis and Ms Gold seemed to be impressed in spite of themselves.

"Splendid!" Ms Gold reached into her pocket and came out with a stick of gum. "No!" I said, and gave him a cookie instead. "Dogs don't chew gum."

Schultz looked disappointed. Riva looked disgusted. Ms. Gold looked as if she had no idea what to ask next. Then, perhaps thinking of her human clients, she asked Riva, "Does he ever get depressed or feel sad?"

Schultz was now doing his second and final party trick: he ran around in wild circles, chasing his tail. Then he stopped, panting, waiting for more praise. I tossed him another cookie.

"Well, he certainly doesn't look sad or depressed," remarked Ms. Gold. "He's very friendly. That indicates an adaptive social attitude. Is he phobic or rebellious or under stress?"

"Of course not. He's a dog, not a person," snapped Riva.

"Yes, of course." Ms Gold seemed to remember whom she was examining, and roused herself to think of more appropriate questions.

"Can you manage to take him out whenever he needs to go?"

Riva nodded.

"Does he bite?"

"Hardly ever," I said.

"Yeah, he does," interjected Noah. "You remember..."

I kicked him. Hard. He rubbed his leg and glared at me, but shut up.

"Is he noisy at night?" Ms. Gold continued.

"No."

"Then he's passed the test! You can stay, Schultz. Congratulations, Mrs. Mannheim," said Ms. Gold.

"Good thing they didn't ask him to heel or sit or lie down or any of the other tricks that most dogs learn in obedience training," I whispered to Riva. "He can't do any of those things."

"He is a very clever dog," said Riva, giving me a nasty stare. She took any criticism of Schultz personally. "He could pass any test."

Right. Any test. I smiled to myself.

With that settled, Ms. Robins seized her chance to get the trio out and distract them from the wreckage in the café. "I have all the accounts in my office," she said. "Shall we look at them?"

But Ms Gold wasn't in a hurry to leave. In fact, she looked quite excited, as if she had made a discovery.

"I understand you've had a few deaths here lately," she said to Ms. Robins. "Your maitre d' died under unusual circumstances too. Throwing tiles and upturning chairs and tables is a definite sign of mental distress and clearly, many residents have been traumatized. That's obvious."

She was getting into her stride, her eyes sparkling, ignoring the fact that the others were getting restless.

"An upturned chair represents the security found in a mother's love, but it also restricts and immobilizes. And what do we have here? Upturned chairs and tables," she said triumphantly. "Of course," she added, "There is also a phallic element to the outstretched legs of the chairs, which is clearly sexual in nature..."

"Huh?" said Noah. "The wrinklies had sex with a chair leg?"

Ms Robins looked furious. She looked ready to throw him out. This was my chance.

"It might have been murder!" I said. But I didn't get the response I had hoped for.

"Yes, of course, dear," said Ms Gold soothingly. To the others, she said, "You see? Trauma, resulting in hysterical confusion. We must deal with this."

That was enough for Ms. Robins, who was chivvying the others to the door. "Out, Noah! You shouldn't be here."

"I propose a serious of therapeutic sessions with the residents, so that they can deal with their feelings about what has happened here," said Ms. Gold, as she regretfully followed the others. Ms. Robins rolled her eyes heavenward. It was easy to tell what she was thinking: What next?

❧ Chapter Twenty ❦

M
s. Gold had had her way and now a therapy session was being held, not in the Vintage Coffee Shop, which she thought would only bring back sad associations, but in the dining room. A space had been cleared in the center of the room, and chairs arranged in a circle. About 20 residents had signed up for the session. Riva hadn't bothered to come, but oddly enough, Josh had asked if he could sit in. I think he wanted to check up on whether I needed therapy.

"*Vos is dos mishugas*?"—"What is this craziness?"—asked Joe Pokroy, an 89-year-old curmudgeon who had shuffled in, grumbling. Most of the others had come along quite willingly. This was something new and anything that broke the tedium was always welcome.

"Where's the food?" Bernice asked.

"We're not here for food; we're here to talk about our feelings," said Ms Gold, who today was wearing a flowing raspberry pink cotton dress and Crocs shoes. Her red hair frizzed out in a halo around her head. It was oddly attractive.

"So why are we in the dining room, if there's no food?"

"Yeah. What's to eat?" The feeling was general. At the Menorah, food was naturally expected on just about every occasion. It was a policy for which I had a lot of sympathy.

Ms Gold seemed to have been caught wrong-footed. A little nervously, she said, "Let me explain. I am a professional therapist.

I'm here to help you cope with the difficulties you might have felt after the deaths of Mr. Levin and Maurice. You might, for example, have felt panic, or had nightmares, or had difficulty functioning. Does anyone want to say anything about that?"

Ah, to be young. I felt like saying that everyone our age had difficulty in functioning from time to time, even without any murders, but I refrained.

"Yes!" said Mollie, waving her hand in the air. "I feel all those things!"

"There, you see? It's the result of trauma."

"It's the result of Mollie being a great big hypochondriac," said Pearl scornfully.

"I am not," said Mollie, irate. "Joyce was the hypochondriac. I'm Nancy Drewski."

Nancy Drewski? Ms. Gold look bewildered, but decided to let it pass, and tried again.

"What were your feelings when you heard about Maurice being locked in the freezer?"

"I felt nauseous," said Dolly. "There was food in that freezer. Maybe we would have to eat it the next day."

A chorus of "ughs," "feh" and "yuks" followed. One woman gagged.

Again, this wasn't quite the reaction Ms. Gold was hoping for.

"I am sure many of you had other feelings. Please, don't feel shy about sharing them. You are not alone!"

"Of course we aren't alone. Look around you—we're all here," said Joe in disgust.

"Maybe the lady can't see so good," offered Mollie.

Bernice got up. "I have to go to the bathroom," she announced. This gave Ms Gold an opening she had been waiting for.

"Thank you Mrs. Baum," she said. "Going to the bathroom at inappropriate times is a clear sign of social anxiety, related to the anal stage and sphincteric phobia. It has obviously been brought on by worry about the sad deaths that have taken place. Would you like to talk about it?

"No. I want to go to the bathroom," said Bernice, as she shuffled out.

"*Narishkeit*!" commented Joe.

"No, it isn't foolishness," snapped Ms. Gold, who to our surprise seemed to know some Yiddish.

Pearl begged to differ. "Bernice has a bladder problem, not a sphincteric phobia, or whatever you call it. This is a waste of time."

There was a murmur of agreement. "And there's no food here either," Sadie Moss said. "A *shandeh*—a disgrace."

"Wouldn't anyone like to talk about the terrible events that have taken place?" Ms Gold asked in some desperation.

Sadie stood up. "I would. My daughter-in-law, she cooked a chicken soup for my son last Friday that I wouldn't serve to a dog. And she had the nerve to tell me to keep quiet when I told her so. Now that was a terrible event."

"Sit down, Sadie. She isn't talking about that kind of terrible event," said Pearl.

In a huff, Sadie sat down. "Well, why doesn't she say so?"

Ms. Gold, who knew she was losing her audience, tried one last tack.

"The chairs and tables that were thrown and turned upside down in the Vintage Café show that your world was turned upside down. We have to analyze why you felt the need to show such violence."

"Why? *Why?* Because Sadie called me a cheater," shouted Norma.

"Norma threw a tile at me and broke my glasses," retorted Sadie.

"I won, but nobody paid me." Bernice had wandered back. It seemed that her lost victory at mahjong still rankled.

It looked like the whole thing was starting again. People were beginning to take sides and voices were being raised. Fortunately, there were no mahjong tiles around to throw, and it was probably a good thing that there was no food either.

Josh looked alarmed. He had been quietly observing, but now he obviously felt the need to put a lid on the incipient uprising.

"People, listen to Ms. Gold. She's just trying to help you."

His negotiation skills may have been effective in business, but here, he was talking to the wall. Ms Gold cast him a grateful look, but everyone else ignored him.

Once again, Ms. Robins came to the rescue.

"What's going on here?" she demanded as she strode into the dining room. The tumult died down to a grumbling murmur.

"We were just finishing," said Ms Gold. "The trauma obviously goes too deep to be concealed and people are voicing their feelings."

But Joe had the last word. "*Narishkeit,*" he said again, shaking his head, as he reached for his cane and shuffled out.

❧ Chapter Twenty-One ❧

I left Josh talking to Ms Gold. He seemed intrigued by her, oddly enough, given the fact that he was usually attracted to busty blonds. When I had asked him why, he said that she reminded him of the girl he had a crush on in third grade. I assumed he planned to quiz Ms Gold on her opinion of my sanity. Well, good luck to him. It would keep him out of my hair. I had lots to do.

Group therapy didn't seem to have shed any light on the murderer at large, so it was time for a new approach. Quizzing Dolly, who had dated Sam, might reveal something.

Dolly seemed to have a grudge against Sam, according to Norma, and when I thought of that piker taking her out for dinner at the Pizzeria and then "forgetting" his wallet at home, I had to admit that I could understand why. Could she have been the one who killed him? Admittedly, if every cheap date in the world were murdered, there would be very few men left. But what the heck. I wasn't going to leave a single stone unturned. I would sound Dolly out.

Dolly wasn't a particular friend of mine, and she certainly wasn't one of Riva's, so it might be a bit odd if I started asking her personal questions off the bat. I would have to think of a tactful way to do it.

I asked Hal and Riva if they had any ideas.

"What's she interested in?" asked Hal.

I was stumped. Dolly didn't play mahjong or bridge. As far as I remembered, she didn't boast overmuch about her grandchildren, or complain too much about her ailments, or kvetch about arrangements in the Menorah. She was just an unobtrusive, elderly woman with seemingly, nothing special about her.

"Wait a minute," said Riva. "Isn't she vegan?"

Many of the residents had special food requirements. Some were diabetic, some kept kosher, a few had allergies and a whole lot were just plain fussy about what they ate. It wasn't uncommon for a resident to be as suspicious of unfamiliar foods as a two-year old. My late husband Manny, for instance, had turned up his nose at any vegetable that wasn't a tomato, dill pickle or wedge of iceberg lettuce. There were a lot of people like that at the Menorah.

But a Jewish senior vegan? That was rare.

I picked up the phone and called the kitchen.

"Tommy, do you cater to any vegans here? Really? What kind of diet is that? Ok, I get the picture. No need to use that kind of language. Thanks."

"Well," I said. "Dolly isn't just a vegan, she's a particularly strict follower of a special diet that's supposed to be really healthy. That means she doesn't eat dairy products, certain fruits, potatoes, legumes, wheat and lots of other stuff. Oh, yes, and nothing processed. Tommy says she insists on checking the labels on all the ingredients he uses before she'll eat anything."

"I gather Tommy doesn't approve."

"That's for sure. He said... well, never mind. But now I know how I can approach Dolly. She knows I like to bake. I'll say that I've decided to bake more healthily and I want her advice."

Hal approved. "That should do it. Just don't expect me to eat the new, improved healthy knishes she persuades you to make."

❧ ☙

"You would like me to show you how to bake healthy things?" Dolly looked doubtful, as well she might, when I approached her. The idea of gluten-free potato knishes made with spelt flour and without potatoes seemed less than appealing.

"Yes," I told her. I leaned closer, as if I were telling her a secret.

"Ms. Robins says I have an ample build. It's time I lost a little weight. I need to learn to cook things that will be good for me."

I waited for her to say that I didn't have an ample build, but I guess no one had taught her the art of the polite lie.

"Well, I suppose I could." She seemed less than enthusiastic, but I let it pass.

"Great! How about cookies? We can make them in my suite and then take them to the kitchen to be baked. I do that all the time."

Dolly thought for a moment. "I used to make vegan oatmeal cookies that were pretty good. I guess I can show you how. I'll look up a list of ingredients, you buy them and we can meet tomorrow. Everything has to be organic, of course."

I gulped when I saw the things I had to buy. Rice bran oil? Non-dairy milk? Golden flax meal? What the heck were these things? And wheatgrass? For cookies? I hope the members of our detective team appreciated the sacrifice I was making in the interests of catching a murderer. I'd had to persuade the driver of the Menorah van to take me to the other end of town to find a health food store that carried this stuff. Dolly had insisted that the raisins had to be free of sulphur dioxide and organic. In fact, everything had to be organic and if possible, locally sourced. Somehow, I doubted that golden flax was grown in Minnesota, particularly at this time of year.

I nibbled on rugelach, which I'd hidden behind the coffee maker, while I waited for Dolly the next day. Might as well enjoy them while I could; there would for sure be no noshing with the health police in my apartment. While I was at it, I hid the sugar container too. Dolly might want to throw it out, if she figured I was a potential convert to her diet.

Schultz scratched at the door and I let him in. I swear, this dog could read minds. He knew that I was planning to bake.

When Dolly appeared, she went right to business, creaming something that passed for butter with something that passed for sugar, and then adding oddly colored grayish brown cranberries and raisins. While she worked, I tried to make conversation.

I started with flattery. In my experience, that usually worked best.

"You look terrific, Dolly," I gushed. "It must be this diet. How do you manage here, with so many forbidden foods on the menu?"

"It's not easy," she replied. "Tommy prepares vegetable plates for me, but he isn't always very helpful. When I asked if the vegetables were locally sourced, he said quite sarcastically that it was hard to find cucumbers from Minnesota in the winter. There was no call for him to talk like that."

She shook her head sorrowfully. "People are just ignorant. They don't know or care that they're eating poison."

Time to get to the point.

"I heard that you went out for pizza with Sam a few weeks ago," I ventured.

"Yes, can you believe it? He asked me out, and then insisted we go for the early bird special at the Pizzeria at 5 o'clock. Naturally I wouldn't touch the pizza. The dough is made from white flour, with gluten. And probably preservatives too." She shuddered.

"Then, when I wanted to explain to him all about the advantages of a healthy diet, he wouldn't listen. He only wanted to talk about some investment he wanted me to make in a firm he was starting. He must think I'm some kind of fool. As if I would trust him with my money! He even made me pay for the meal with the phony excuse that he forgot his wallet at home."

Bingo. He was after her money.

"You must have been furious. Did you think he was romantically interested in you when he asked you out?" I asked.

Dolly laughed. She rolled the dough into balls, which she placed on a cookie sheet. One piece of dough dropped on the floor. Schultz sniffed at it, left it untouched and walked away. He looked disgruntled and scratched at the door again, to be let out. I knew what he was thinking. I felt like that too.

Lining up the trays on the counter, Dolly said, "I don't know if he was romantically interested in me, but I certainly wasn't turned on by him. I could never be interested in someone who has such terrible food habits. Sure I was mad, at first, but after I thought about it, I found the whole business funny. It made a good story."

She certainly didn't sound like a killer. In fact, except for her love of wheatgrass and rice bran oil, she sounded like a woman with a lot of good common sense; so much good sense that I decided to feel her out on our murder theory.

"Do you think someone killed Sam and Maurice?"

"No, of course not. Nobody here would do anything like that. Why would they?"

"Maybe Sam was blackmailing somebody."

"Sam? That old fool? Who would he be blackmailing, anyway? Nobody here has anything to hide. I think you're letting your imagination run away with you, Ellie. Now, to get back to the diet, have you tried kale? It's delicious with quinoa. I don't know why you insist on making things like knishes and blintzes. So bad for your immune system."

Dolly may not have been the murderer, but she had come up with one useful fact: Sam was trying to persuade women into putting their money into an iffy investment scheme. It sounded that as well as going in for blackmail and false declarations of love, he was a con man trying to get people to invest in a dodgy company. Was there a gullible woman or man who had invested money in his firm, and then, after the money was lost, decided to kill him? I was eager to get rid of Dolly and share these new thoughts with Riva and Hal.

"Thanks so much," I told her, easing her towards the door. "I'll just get these cookies to the kitchen to bake."

With Dolly gone, I reached behind the coffee maker for the hidden rugelach. Fortunately, Dolly hadn't seen them. I took a welcome bite of the delicious confection, poison though it might be. I thought of tipping the contents of the freshly prepared cookie tray straight into the rubbish bin, but then I thought again. Who knows? I could be adventurous. They might actually be tasty.

❧ Chapter Twenty-Two ❧

S am was a man of many talents," I said to Hal. It was later that day, and I was in the Community Archive again, sharing the latest information with Riva and Hal. Noah had come along too. Josh, to my surprise, was still with Ms Gold. He had mentioned that she was going to read him some of the poetry she had written. It would make a change from his usual reading matter—the Wall Street Journal.

"Sam had many talents? Really? What talents did he have, besides juggling and blackmailing?"

"Apparently, he was an all-purpose con man. Dolly said that he was trying to get her to invest in some business he had. As far as I know, that business was nothing but monkey business. He picked the wrong mark in Dolly, but he probably tried it with other people too. Suppose he got someone to invest their life savings in his business, and then said the money was lost? That would certainly be a motive for murder. How can we find out?"

Hal poured me a cup of coffee from the machine and handed it to me, along with some stale crackers he took out of a package. I made a mental note to bring him some more home-baked cookies.

"What about getting Noah to look around in his computer files again? He might find some information about this business, or maybe false receipts or contracts," he said.

Schultz barked.

"Well, here's someone who thinks that's a good idea," I said. "Can you do it, Noah?"

"Whatcha think, Bubbie? I told you I know his log-in address. I can use the computer here."

Tossing a few sticks of gum in his mouth for inspiration, Noah sat down at one of the office computers and quickly clicked in to Sam's personal account. "So what do you wanna know? What he spent on on-line poker? His e-mails? His 'Finances' file? 'Business'?"

"Try 'Business,'" said Hal. We crowded around the computer. Noah called up a letter, which had a quite impressive letterhead logo. It was an invitation to invest in a firm called Cambridge Research Investments Inc.—"good name", Hal remarked—which Sam represented, and which claimed to be a pharmaceutical start-up that was developing a cure for the common cold. ("No less!") It promised that once research had been completed and the Food and Drug Administration had approved the drug, the return on investment would be in the level of 1000%.

"Who would believe such a story?"

"The same people who buy shares in the Brooklyn Bridge or vacant land in Florida that's just about to be redeveloped, or who invested with Bernie Madoff," said Hal.

"I believed Madoff," Riva said, unexpectedly. "I thought he was a nice Jewish man. Even the Hadassah organization invested with him, so I did too. I am lucky that I have enough left to live here."

That was revealing. It may have explained why Riva was so remote and suspicious of everyone. But still, Sam was no Madoff. It was hard to believe that anyone would go for the story of a cure for the common cold.

Did the computer files show anything?

Noah tapped away, looking for a clue. "Here's a copy of a letter that Sam wrote. It's a kind of a blank receipt for investing in Cambridge Research Investment Co. I can't tell if he actually sent this receipt, or just prepared it in case anyone gave him money to invest.

"Hey! Here's a list of prospects. There are lots of people from the Menorah here—I see Joyce Kramer's name and also Pearl Green, Sadie Diamond, Norma Vogel, Dolly Klein, Julius Diamond... lots of people."

"But those are just prospects. He planned to approach them,

but he may not have, and even if he did, they may not have gone for his scheme," I pointed out.

"True. We'll have to sound each of them out.

"Maybe you should ask around, Ellie."

"Oh, no. Does that mean I have to play mahjong again?"

"Maybe, "said Riva. "But you can start asking around with Pearl. Sam might have approached her, because she's wealthy."

"Why don't you ever try to pump anyone, Riva?" I grumbled. "Why do I have to do it?"

"Because it is out of character for me. Everyone knows that I seldom talk to anyone," she said, with some complacency.

"How very convenient for you," I couldn't resist saying.

Riva looked put out. She didn't like criticism. She was the one with the insults, not me.

"Well, if you don't want to find out who murdered Sam and Mollie, then you do not need to be part of this."

"Hey, hey, Marplestein and Shoirlock, no fighting," said Hal. "The next thing you know, you'll be throwing mahjong tiles. Let's get with the program, as our young friend Noah says."

"Yeah, get with the program. I can ask people, if you don't want to, Bubbie," offered Noah.

"No! I'll do it, I'll do it. But I won't like it.

☙ ❧

The best way to start, I thought, was just to come out with it.

"Pearl," I said casually, over lunch that day, "Did Sam ever mention investing in a company he had?"

Pearl sniffed. (She sniffed a lot. People who think they're better than anyone else tend to do that, I've noticed.)

"Yes, he certainly did. He tried to get me to invest in a company that was going to find a cure for the common cold. He must have thought that I was an idiot. My son does all my investing. Not the son who's a doctor; the other one."

"We know. The one who is a lawyer," said Riva poker-faced. I poked her under the table. Antagonizing Pearl was not going to help us get the information we needed.

"Do you think he tried to convince anyone else to invest in his company?"

"How would I know? I don't poke my nose into people's business, like some people," she said, glaring at Riva and me.

"He asked me," said Bernice, in a small voice.

"Sam asked you to invest?" I said, horrified. "But you didn't do it, did you?"

"Bernice, were you stupid enough to give him money?" Pearl snapped. "How could you be such a fool?"

Bernice sniffed and reached in her pocket for a tissue. "Yes, I did. He said if I invested a few thousand dollars, I would get lots more back when the cure the scientists were working on started selling. Then he died, and when I asked his son about it, he didn't know what I was talking about."

She was crying in earnest now. Then, clutching her tissue, she ran off towards the washroom.

"Let her go," said Pearl. "She'll forget all about it soon enough, and she won't miss the money. I don't know why I bother with her. Tommy!" she called, as he passed by. "Bernice won't be having dessert. And by the way, I had to wait a long time for my meal. Things were much better when Maurice was around."

Tommy, not as diplomatic as Maurice, didn't deign to answer and walked on, gritting his teeth. I got up to follow Bernice and see how she was doing. But this exchange had given us something to think about. Not only was Bernice possibly being blackmailed, but she had fallen for an investment pitch that had lost her what could be a substantial sum of money. Could that helpless pose be a cover? Could a woman who could barely control her bladder manage to murder Sam, not to mention Maurice?

In the restroom, I put my arm around Bernice, who was sobbing again because Pearl had been mean to her. No, I was convinced, a woman who was so distressed by a silly comment couldn't possibly have the will to plan a complicated murder. We would have to strike poor Bernice off the list of potential killers.

My dreams were fitful again that night. I seemed to be stuck in a snow bank, with a church bell ringing... could it be Christmas? No, it was the telephone ringing. I looked at my bedside clock. It was 3 am. Who would be calling me at this hour? In a panic, I thought of the grandchildren. Had something happened? I grabbed for the receiver.

"Yes?"

The voice was raspy and clearly disguised: "I'm warning you. Mind your own business, or you'll be the next one to go," the voice croaked. It was impossible to tell if it was a man or a woman, or even young or old. It sounded like a person who could use Sam's company's cure for the common cold.

Surprisingly, I wasn't frightened, possibly because the speaker seemed to be following the script of a bad television detective show. What cliché would he—or she—produce now? I waited for the line "Don't do anything stupid, like call the cops," and sure enough, that's what came next. I felt like giggling. I knew I had to keep the speaker on the line, to try to find out who was threatening me.

"Who are you?" I asked. It wasn't a very original line, but the best I could do at this time of the night.

"Never mind. Just stay out of it, you and Riva and that *meshugganeh* dog. Or you'll be sorry." The phone went dead.

Well, that was revealing. The threatening voice had to belong to someone who knew Yiddish expressions, and that meant one of the residents. Also someone who liked bad detective novels. Unless, of course, the murderer wasn't a resident at all and had tossed in the phrase "*meshugganeh*" to throw me off the scent. I sighed.

It was all too much. I looked again at the list of suspects that Riva and I had compiled, crumpled it up and threw it in the wastepaper basket. I couldn't sleep anymore, so I got out of bed wearily, went to the fridge and inspected what ingredients I had, quietly, so as not to disturb Josh. Fortunately, he had always been a heavy sleeper.

Flour, check. Butter, check. Nuts, check. Eggs, check. Great. I could do it. If I prepared the dough for mandelbrot biscuits now, I could take them to be baked when the kitchen opened at 7 am. That is, assuming I could keep my eyes open. I went back to the bedroom, with the flour sack in my hands and sat down on the bed. My eyelids closed. I would just rest for a minute or two... and then, I jumped. Someone was knocking at the door. Could it be Mr. or Ms. Raspy Voice, ready to do me in?

Of course it wasn't. It was now 9 am and Riva and Hal were at the door. They looked relieved to see me, although a little surprised to find a small pyramid of spilled flour on my bed. Josh stirred, got up and went into the bathroom. Good. I didn't want him to hear what my friends had to say.

"You aren't even dressed and you missed breakfast," Riva said in an accusing tone. "You never miss a meal. I was worried. I asked Hal to come over."

Hal said nothing, but he didn't need to. I knew what was in his mind. He didn't think I could take care of myself.

I yawned and stretched. "I fell asleep after someone woke me up at 3 o'clock in the morning with a threat. I couldn't tell who was calling, because the voice was disguised, but whoever it was told me to mind my own business, or I would be the next one killed. It was all a little ridiculous, like someone following a script. A bad script."

"You aren't taking this seriously enough," said Hal. "This guy isn't a joker—he's already killed a few people. This is definitely something we could report to the police."

"And have Johnson and Smyth tell me that I dreamed it? Nope. You know they think I'm gaga."

"Well, we could tell Ms. Robins. They would believe her."

"No," said Riva. "Ms. Robins is still a suspect."

Josh, in the shower, was now singing tunelessly. Was that song "The Age of Aquarius" I heard? Could my entrepreneurial son be turning into a hippy, after only one session with Ms Gold?

Hal brought me back to the matter at hand.

"It's pointless just wondering aimlessly who the murderer is. We need to get organized and develop a plan," said Hal. "Time we had another strategy meeting, in view of the latest developments."

Riva, the ex-school principal, liked that idea. Organization was right up her street. "You write this down, Ellie."

Yes, boss.

"Let us consider all the suspects." She ticked them off. "Ms. Robins was being blackmailed by Sam. She admits it. She is a definite suspect."

"But," I said, "her son is dependent on her. She wouldn't have wanted to take any chances of getting caught and sent to prison."

"I don't agree, Ellie," said Hal. "She might have figured that it was worth taking the chance. Sam would have kept on blackmailing her. She had motive, opportunity and means. And she's smart. She's definitely still on the list."

"Sam was blackmailing Maurice too, and possibly someone

else. Maurice could have killed him."

"But then," I said, "who killed Maurice?"

True. We were back where we started.

"Bernice is also a suspect," Riva said. "She had a motive—she had invested in Sam's firm and lost her money—and she also had the means and the opportunity. When she claimed she was going to the bathroom, she could have been going to the kitchen to plant a pill in the knishes and to do in Maurice."

"She may have had a motive, but she has no brains," said Hal.

"Maybe she's just pretending to be clueless?" I suggested.

We all laughed. "I'd prefer Schultz as a suspect. He's a lot cleverer, right boy? Also, he had motive—Sam didn't like him—and opportunity. He was right there when it all happened."

Schultz barked, pleased at the attention.

Riva, as usual, was impatient with all the pleasantries. "Let us not waste time. There are many suspects, if we include the names on the list of prospects to invest in his scheme that Sam had on his computer—Julius, Joyce, Sadie, Norma. There were others too. I can't remember all their names, but any of them could have wished Sam dead, if he had stolen their money."

"Don't forget Dolly," I said. "She claims that she was amused by Sam, but he did humiliate her. She could be just pretending to be innocent. She's definitely smart and tough enough to be a killer."

"She smothered him to death with flax meal," said Hal with a grin. "Or maybe she drowned him in organic non-dairy milk."

I grinned back. "She threw sulphur dioxide-free raisins at him and knocked him flat out."

Hal was caught up in the game. "He choked to death on kale."

"Stop this nonsense."

"Right, Ms Marplestein, We'll be serious," said Hal. He winked at me.

"We have to sound each of our suspects out. You were supposed to ask around, Ellie."

"I did. I started with Pearl. She said Sam did approach her, but she told him that her son did all her investing. Then we got sidetracked by Bernice. Pearl never did tell me if she knew anybody else who had been asked to invest."

"So what now?"

We were stumped again.

❧ Chapter Twenty-Three ❧

Josh and I spent the day tooling around town in his snazzy Porsche and shopping. We bought baking supplies for me and a yoga mat for him—Ms Gold's influence again—and then stopped for lunch at a chic new place, where they treated us deferentially and seated us right by the window. That was the advantage of being a youngish, good-looking guy and a Porsche owner; you got treated with respect, unlike people of my age, who were generally treated in restaurants as if we were semi-invisible and seated next to the kitchen or the restroom.

I could get used to this. The lunch was delicious.

After Josh dropped me off at home, I pondered the question of Bernice. Try as I might, I just couldn't see her as a murderer. She was simply too helpless—a victim, not a killer, and she wasn't cold blooded. It couldn't be an act. So if not her, who was the killer? And why?

Everyone now seemed to know that Riva and I were involved in some detective work, thanks to Mollie, so did that mean that we were in danger too? What could we do about it, other than keep Schultz around as a watchdog. I sighed. Not much.

The phone rang and I jumped. This whole business was making me nervous.

"Hi Shoirlock." It was Hal. He'd never telephoned me before. "Any news?"

"Well, it seems that Bernice was investing with Sam. She lost all her money, of course. She had reason to wish Sam dead, but, I don't know, I just don't think she has the moxie to commit murder, let alone being capable. What do you think?"

"Same as you. Whoever killed Sam planned it carefully. That kind of planning would be far beyond Bernice's capabilities. Uh…" he paused. What now?

"Would you like to discuss this over dinner tonight?" said Hal.

"You mean you want to come here for dinner? I could make knishes."

"No, Ellie. I mean that I want the two of us to go out for dinner."

Was he asking me out on a date? I couldn't believe this. I didn't even know if the term "date" still existed. I would have to ask Noah. Since the last date I'd been on was before my marriage, 45 years ago, I was hardly an expert.

My hand was shaking. I dropped the phone with a clatter. Me? A date? With Hal? I fumbled for the receiver, hoping he hadn't heard the clunk and said, "Sorry Hal. Sure, that would be great."

"I'll pick you up at 7. See you then."

He didn't intend to take me out for the early bird special, then. This was class. I had to tell Riva right away!

"He asked me out!" I said, after she let me into her apartment. "What should I wear? Should I get my hair done, or will that look like I'm trying too hard. But if I don't get my hair done, it will look awful and it will look like I'm not trying at all. Maybe I shouldn't go. I could just stay home and bake something."

"Riva, what should I do?" I wrung my hands.

"Act your age, Ellie. You are being embarrassing."

"Are you crazy? My age is exactly what I don't want to act like. Who's interested in an old lady?"

"Well, don't act like a lovesick teenager. You will go of course, and wear something nice. A dress, not pants. And you will get your hair done. It may not improve your appearance, but you will feel better."

I smiled. "You know me too well, Riva."

But now, I had another worry.

"What will we talk about? Maybe I should ask Noah what people talk about on dates these days?"

Riva burst into laughter. Schultz looked up to see what the

joke was.

"Ask Noah? He will tell you that teenagers don't even talk. They just send messages to each other. They probably also consider 'date' to be an outmoded turn. They just 'hook up'."

The thought of hooking up, if it meant what I thought it meant, made me gulp. Surely that wasn't what Hal had in mind? No, he couldn't possibly. Could he? I wasn't sure if that were a good thing or a bad thing. For sure, it was a scary thing.

"I wish you could come with me, Riva."

"No you don't."

True. I didn't really. I just needed someone to give me a little self-confidence, and Riva was the best I had. For a fleeting moment, I thought of taking the dog along. Then, if things weren't going well, I could say the dog needed a walk. How bizarre would that be? (Very bizarre.) I dismissed that idea. I would manage—or not, as the case may be—on my own.

Riva rolled her eyes, as if she thought my idea of bringing her along was too stupid to even comment on, which it was.

"I have plans of my own tonight," she said. "I will go over to the Community Archive when it's quiet and look around. Maybe there is some file that is relevant to the murders. Hal can give me the key."

"By yourself?

"Of course by myself. Who should I take with me, Bernice?"

I was doubtful. "It's really cold outside and the sidewalks are icy. Are you sure you can manage to get there alone?"

"Don't patronize me, Ellie," she said tartly. "I've been managing on my own for many years. I will take my walker, and I assure you, I can manage to get there and back safely. I can read the files better without you and Hal to distract me. The dog will come with me."

I wasn't happy about it, but there was no arguing with her. What could the dog possibly do if she were in trouble? Drag her home?

In any case, I had other important things to think about—like whether wearing a black dress would be a bad thing because it would make my wrinkles more prominent, or whether it would be a good thing, because it would make me look slimmer.

In the end, I opted for a black dress with a red scarf at the neck; thus, in theory, looking slimmer and at the same time, disguising my wrinkles. Or maybe the opposite. Whatever. The last time I had worn the dress was to my grandson's bar mitzvah, back in 1998. It was loose then and it was snug now, but at least it fit, more or less. Come to think of it, the last time I had had an actual date, Lyndon Johnson was President.

❧ ❦

"You look very nice," said Hal, when he came to collect me.

"You look nice too." And he did. Hal was wearing a sports jacket and a tie, and had obviously shaved for the occasion, because there was a fresh nick on his chin. I don't know what aftershave he used, but he smelled good too. I was pleased that I had worn a fancy-schmancy outfit. So what if it looked like I was making an effort. I was!

It was a little awkward introducing Hal to Josh, naturally. When I'd asked Josh if he minded if I left him that evening because I was going out, he had been incredulous.

"You're going out with a guy?"

No, I felt like replying, with a dog. But I kept my mouth shut. No doubt it was difficult for Josh to believe that his ancient mother actually had a social life that didn't revolve around *shiva* calls in the library and monthly birthday parties.

"Yes," I told him. "The fellow who works in the Community Archive has invited me for dinner. We're friends."

"Really?" To give him credit, he seemed pleased.

"Well, I'll have to check him out," he teased.

That made me nervous. I had hoped that he would be doing yoga or something. The last thing I needed was my son casting a critical eye at Hal. What would Hal think? On the other hand, I couldn't help but feel proud that I had someone as impressive as Hal to show off to Josh. And of course, someone as impressive as my darling Josh to show off to Hal.

As for leaving him alone in the suite, that was no problem, Josh said, because he had arranged to talk some more with Ms Gold.

Although Josh and Hal, on the face of it, had little in common but me, the two of them seemed to hit it off, particularly when Hal

138

started by complimenting me.

"Your mom is quite a girl."

"She is? I mean, yes, she is!" Hal wasn't used to thinking of me as anything other than his devoted, and occasionally irritating, elderly mother. I think I had just gone up in his estimation.

I felt a pang of guilt. Josh had come all the way from New York to see me, and here I was leaving him alone in a retirement home.

"What are you planning to talk about with Ms. Gold? I asked Josh. "There's a good movie in the dining room."

Hal laughed. "Yeah, I saw the notice. No, I don't really want to see the Marx Brothers, but don't worry about me. I have plans. So, have a good time, Mom."

Please Josh, don't embarrass me by saying 'Don't do anything I wouldn't do.'

"Don't do anything I wouldn't do!"

I clenched my teeth. Hal grinned. On that note, we left, and passed through the lobby where a row of ladies sitting on the sofa looked at us with great interest. Through the open door of the Vintage cafe, I saw the mahjong ladies also staring at our departure. Ms. Robins, who was still in her office, raised her eyebrows and then waved.

Would anybody actually say something? What a question. Does it snow in winter in Minnesota? Of course, everyone would comment.

"Where are you going Ellie?" asked Mollie. "You're wearing makeup."

"I think she had her hair done too," Sadie piped up.

The others eagerly waited to hear what I would have to say. I was momentarily stumped.

Hal filled the breach. "We're going to a Hadassah dinner," he said, with a pleasant smile. Hadassah is a Jewish women's charitable association that is very popular among retirees. Many of the Menorah residents belonged.

As we left, I heard the buzz start.

"Hadassah dinner? What Hadassah dinner? I wasn't invited to a dinner."

It was icy outside and beginning to snow, and as Hal took my arm, I burst out laughing. "You're terrible. Sadie is now going to give up her membership in Hadassah because she wasn't invited to the dinner."

"They'll figure it out," said Hal. I was still chuckling as he helped me into his car. The exchange had broken the ice. I wasn't nervous anymore. I was just Shoirlock, out for dinner with her friend Vatson and having a good time.

We drove to L'Auberge, an elegant French restaurant, where the food was about as far from the early bird special at the Pizzeria as you could get. After the frigid wind outside, nothing could be more welcoming than this room, with its blazing wood fire, pleasant buzz of conversation, clink of wine glasses and aroma of delicious food. I couldn't think of a pleasanter place to be.

"This is nice," Hal remarked, as the waiter filled my glass with white wine.

"Yes, it is," I said. "And to make it even nicer, let's agree, for once, not to talk about the murders."

"Fine with me. What shall we talk about? Books? Films? Gossip? What you want to be when you grow up?

"It's funny that you should mention growing up," I said. "Riva keeps telling me that I'm acting like a child, particularly when I do something she considers foolhardy and thoughtless."

"I don't think you act like a child. A little reckless, perhaps, but your heart is in the right place. I'm sorry, by the way, that I've been so bossy. I know I have that tendency. It comes from being a teacher to a bunch of unruly kids. I'm working on it." He filled my glass again.

"Here's to staying young!" We both laughed. This was fun. Time was passing so pleasantly.

Our food came—a luscious terrine, followed by pot au feu and for dessert, crepes with brandy. I was in heaven. Comfort food, French style—perfect for a stormy night.

"This certainly makes a change from the Jewish-style food you like to prepare," Hal said.

"Well, yes, of course, it's French, but still, every culture has variations on the same things. This pot au feu is similar to Jewish cholent. The pate bears a family relationship to chopped liver. The crepes—well, think of blintzes."

"And knishes, of course, are related to empanadas and samosas. But better," he said gallantly.

"Thank you," I said, smiling. But mention of knishes had brought Sam's hideous death to mind again. We couldn't seem to escape it, although we tried.

"Uh, uh. Let's not talk about knishes. Bad memories. So... when you were younger, what did you want to be when you grew up?" He poured me another glass of wine.

"I always wanted to be a teacher, and that's what I became," said Hal. 'It's not the easiest job in the world, but I always felt that if I could make a difference to a kid's life, my life would be worthwhile. You don't become rich as a teacher, but we always had enough. I figured I was a lucky guy, until Annie got sick. I was devastated when she died. What about you? What did you want to do?"

"Shamefully, nothing much," I said. "In my younger days, most girls just didn't have the ambitions that they do today. Not that young women didn't work, but if they did decide to, they were generally expected to become social workers or teachers or secretaries. Actually, what most of us really wanted was to get married. I'm embarrassed to admit it, but that was my ambition too. I got married to the first guy who asked me. I was only 19. To tell the truth, it wasn't the best marriage in the world. Manny was a gambler and I suspect he had women on the side, but what could I do? I had no skills and my parents were poor and couldn't help me. In a sense, I think I'm just growing up now."

"And what do you want to do, now that you're grown up?"

"Maybe become a detective! But here we are, back to the murders we weren't going to discuss. We can't seem to get away from the subject. On that note, it's getting late."

He looked at his watch. "Wow, time has passed quickly. It's after 10." He called for the bill.

"I had a wonderful time. We must do this again soon," he said, reaching for my hand.

"I did too."

We didn't say much on the way home, but the silence was comfortable. It was plain that we liked one another. As for the future, well, maybe we would be friends, maybe something more. Neither of us was in a rush—in spite of our ages.

"Would you like some coffee?" I asked him. It occurred to me that no one would be in the entrance hall at this hour, so we wouldn't have to run the *yenta* gauntlet. But surprisingly, the entrance hall was crowded. Even Ms. Robins was there, although it was way past the usual time she left for the night. Schultz was dashing around in circles. I looked for Riva, but she wasn't there. This wasn't good. She never let Schultz out on his own.

"Oh, there you are," said Ms. Robins, looking grave. "Can you take care of the dog? Mrs. Mannheim has had a small accident. She was outside and her walker skidded on some ice and she fell down."

A small accident? I felt a chill at my heart.

"Was she badly hurt?"

Ms Robins patted me reassuringly. "Don't worry. Riva knocked herself unconscious, but the doctors say she didn't break any bones. She's in the hospital now. I think you'll be allowed to see her, if you want to."

Of course I wanted to, and so did Hal. Stopping only to take Schultz up to my suite and to change my shoes for boots, we drove to the hospital, which was only about a mile away. It was midnight now, but the nurse on duty allowed us to see her briefly.

Riva looked small and frail in the hospital bed, but her spirit was as feisty as ever.

"How are you, you silly woman? I told you the ice was treacherous." I asked, trying to hug her. She pushed me away.

"Don't fuss, Ellie," she said. "I am fine. Ms. Robins called an ambulance and they insisted I come here for observation, because they thought I might have a concussion, but I was only shaken up. They are making a big to-do about nothing."

"But it might have been something," said Hal. "It was very foolish of you to go out on such a stormy night by yourself."

"Ellie is right. You are bossy," she said acerbically. "I was wearing strong boots and with my walker, I have a good sense of balance. I have never fallen before. I didn't tell Ms. Robins, but I think someone may have tampered with my walker."

The walker was in the room and Hal and I examined it. On the face of it, the walker looked quite normal. It had a lightweight aluminum frame in a U-shape, with four legs. The two front legs had wheels, while the two back legs had skid-proof caps on the bottoms. Hal peered at the wheels.

"Looks normal," he said. Then he turned the walker upside down. He ran his hand over the bottom of the caps on the back legs. "They're slippery," he said. "Are they usually slippery like this, Riva?"

"No, they are very stable. They have to be."

"Then I think they must have been waxed or oiled. It's no wonder you fell outside."

"I knew it." Riva winced as she maneuvered herself in bed to get a better look at the walker. She may have been making light of her fall, but I had no doubt that she would have a few aches and pains as souvenirs of this adventure.

"Who knew you were going to the Community Archive?" I asked.

"I mentioned it at dinner, and I also told Ms. Robins and signed out at the desk. Many people knew."

"And you leave your walker outside your door, so anyone could have fiddled with it," Hal said. "Did Schultz bark while you were in your suite after supper, before you went out?"

"Yes, now that you mention it, he did. But he often barks when people are outside my door, so I didn't think anything of it." Her eyelids drooped and she leaned back against the pillows.

"You're exhausted," I said. "We'll leave you now. Call me in the morning when the doctor has been to look at you, and I'll come and take you home. In the meantime, don't worry about Schultz. He's quite happy with me."

'I'm sure he is. You always feed him things that are not good for him, Ellie." But her eyes were closing, and Hal and I crept away.

"Now you have to believe that there's a murderer around," I said.

"Well, I haven't been absolutely sure, but now I'm convinced. Someone wanted to stop Riva from investigating in the Community Archive and they almost succeeded. There's definitely someone dangerous on the loose."

&· Chapter Twenty-Four ·&

It was a wild night again, with the kind of storm you get in Minnesota in the winter, a high wind, snow flurries and branches lashing the windows. Normally, I enjoyed a good storm, provided I was indoors, but now I couldn't sleep. It seemed that others couldn't either, because I heard footsteps outside in the hall and a door banging. Eventually, I dropped off and woke to a bright, cold morning. Josh was fast asleep. The sun was out and the snow was piled high, white and clean. It drove away the terrors of the night before and made my worries seem inconsequential.

Maybe Sam did drop dead of a heart attack, and the pill meant nothing. Maybe the door to the freezer did shut by accident on Maurice. Maybe Riva had just slipped. Maybe I was being ridiculous pretending to be a Jewish version of Sherlock Holmes. What did I need this for? Anyway, I was hungry.

On my way to the dining room, I noticed that Mollie wasn't on the sofa in the lobby, though Ms. Robins was in her office. She seemed to have pulled herself together and was as neat and packaged as ever. She gave me a frosty smile. It appeared that her strategy was to pretend that the meeting the day before hadn't happened.

Riva was at breakfast, I was delighted to see. She hadn't waited for me to pick her up, and with her usual "don't fuss" mentality had called a taxi to take her back from the hospital.

I was the last one at our table, and I glanced around the dining room for Mollie, whose place was empty. It wasn't like her to sleep in. "Have you seen Mollie this morning," I asked.

Bernice looked blank. Pearl said, "She's probably in the lobby, checking up on everybody."

"No, she's not," I said. It worried me a bit. Maybe our adventure tailing Ms. Robins had been too much for her.

Riva understood what I was thinking. Could Mollie's irrepressible curiosity and big mouth, possibly have made her another target?

"We will go see when we have finished our breakfast."

For once, my appetite had disappeared.

"Let's go now, Riva," I urged. I felt my chest tighten.

Mollie's door was unlocked, but I was reluctant to let myself in. I knocked on the door, first quietly, then more urgently. No answer. Schultz growled and pawed at the door as Katerine wheeled her service wagon down the hall towards us.

"Would you please get Ms. Robins?" I asked her, my voice shaking.

She looked alarmed, but asked no questions and ran to the elevator. Riva and I waited in silence..

Within five minutes, Ms. Robins was there. She said nothing as she opened the door. We followed her into the room. Mollie lay on the sofa, one leg bent under her, her eyes staring. Her blue eyes, still ringed by eye shadow, stared vacantly. The television was on. Ironically, it was screening a detective program. A cup of tea had spilled on the coffee table next to the sofa, and the liquid had dripped on the rug. Other than that, and a sofa pillow on the floor, everything was just as it should be.

Ms. Robins felt Mollie's pulse. "She's passed away quite peacefully, watching television. Your adventure the other day must have been too much for her heart." She glanced at me reproachfully. "The noise of the storm probably drowned out any cry she might have made."

"Don't be too upset," she added, looking at Riva, who was leaning on her walker, her face grey. "She was in her 90s, and she enjoyed life right to the end. I'll get a doctor to confirm her death."

Left alone, I said to Riva, "I don't believe she died naturally. She was full of energy yesterday and didn't seem at all sick."

Riva nodded. "You're right. It's far too suspicious, Mollie died just after telling everyone in the lobby that we suspected Sam had been murdered. The murderer might be getting panicky and thought she knew more than she actually did."

"What is it, Schultz?" The dog was nosing around the pillow that had fallen off the sofa. I picked it up. The back of the pillow was smeared with bright red lipstick. The most likely way that could have happened was for someone to have forced the pillow onto Mollie's face and smothered her. It wouldn't have been difficult—she was a small woman, and unsuspecting. She would have let someone that she knew into her suite. That was why the door had been unlocked.

Riva, usually so upright, so sure of herself, suddenly looked like what she was—an old woman. I put my arm around her.

"The first thing we have to do is persuade the police that a post-mortem needs to be done. The second thing is to keep people here from gossiping. Three people have died already, and we might be next. And the third thing is to find out who did it."

"Ellie, I didn't think you had this strength in you," said Riva. "You are stronger than I am. You don't give up."

No. I didn't.

☙ ❧

Once again a death. Once again a *shiva*. But while Sam's *shiva* had been a social occasion, this one was truly sad. Everyone felt it, even the staff. With the death of Mollie, the soul seemed to have gone out of the Menorah.

Mollie's two children had passed away before her and the mourners were three grandchildren who looked to be in their 40s and a half dozen great-grandchildren. We knew the family, since most of them lived locally and often visited, and of course the accomplishments of the great-grandchildren, particularly 16-year-old Jill, were a frequent topic of conversation for Mollie.

Everyone, it went without saying, had come to the *shiva*. The sorrow was genuine.

My Josh had come too, since he had met, and been entertained by, Mollie on previous visits. I noticed that he and Ms Gold, who had also come to the *shiva*, had gravitated towards one another.

"I want to say something." Jill, a high-schooler whose academic accomplishments had been frequently touted by Mollie, spoke up. Her voice quavered, and she crushed a tissue in her hand.

"I know a lot of you thought that my Bubbie was a bit odd, and she was."

Smiles all around.

"She acted like a young person and she dressed like one. Sometimes she looked a bit silly. I remember when she put a blue streak in her hair because Lady Gaga had one. Fortunately, that didn't last long. My mom said she was glad it wasn't a tattoo!

"My Bubbie liked to gossip and some people criticized her for it, but she was interested in people, in a good way, and if she found out that anyone needed help, she would be the first in line to offer it. I'll tell you a story: You know those charity appeals that come in the mail all the time? My Bubbie wasn't rich, but she donated to every single one. Even when we told her that some of them were bogus, she would say, 'If nine of them are phony and one isn't, I should ignore that one? Better to give to them all.' That was typical of her good heart.

"If she were here, she would tell you that she loved living in the Menorah and she was sad that people were leaving. She felt lucky to be here. Her message would be: 'Enjoy life. Be grateful for what you have. Don't run away.'"

At that, Jill collapsed in sobs in her father's arms.

Noah, who had of course come to the *shiva*, seemed struck by Jill's eulogy. I couldn't tell what he was saying to her, but it couldn't have been too tactless, because Jill was smiling through her tears. The two of them moved to a corner, talking intently. Well how about that? Maybe she would teach him manners. I thought, and wished Noah wouldn't say or do anything too stupid and spoil his chances, though knowing Noah, it seemed a vain hope.

Ms. Robins stood up. "I have something to say too."

"Now what?" muttered Pearl.

For once, Ms. Robins looked hesitant. She had recovered from her breakdown of the day before, and was as competently turned out as ever. But something had changed.

"What Jill says is true. Mollie was a good person and we will all miss her terribly. Yes, even I will. I know that some of you find me a bit strict"—everybody nodded—"and that has been a mistake on my part. From now on, things are going to change. I will still run the Menorah to the best of my ability, but I have learned something from Mollie. No, I won't be wearing muu-muus"— smiles again—"but I will try to be more accepting, more tolerant, more patient. And I do hope that anyone who is thinking of leaving the Menorah will think again.

"There is nothing to be afraid of. The police have investigated thoroughly and they have concluded that Sam and Mollie died naturally and Maurice died accidentally. Let's all go back to enjoying the Menorah and all that it has to offer. Mollie would have wanted that."

It seemed to work. People seemed calmer and no one was inclined to argue. I heard Sadie say, "I'm going to try to persuade Joyce to come back."

"What do you think, Riva?" I whispered to her.

"I think that something good may have come out of this sad death if it changes the way Ms. Robins behaves, but I still think that someone murdered all three of them. And I am not letting Ms. Robins off the hook."

I had to agree. "We should have get together to decide on our next step. You call Hal and I'll speak to Noah, although he seems pretty occupied by Jill. We'll have a meeting tomorrow in the Community Archive, so that no one here will see us."

"Ellie," said Riva sadly. "No one is going to see. The only one who would really care is dead."

She was right. It was as if the ghost of Mollie had flitted across the scene, a big lipsticked smile on her face and her Nancy Drew beret lopsided on her hair.

Farewell Nancy Drewski. I hoped there was a comfortable sofa in heaven, conveniently near the pearly gates.

❧ Chapter Twenty-Five ❧

Something ominous was going on in the Archive. The secret of the deaths that haunted the Menorah lay here, I was sure. It was where Ms. Robins had learnt about her grandfather, and where Sam had found out her secret and blackmailed her. It was where Sam had evidently learned something that led him to blackmail someone else. And it was where someone had tried to prevent Riva from investigating. That person may well have killed Sam. So what had Sam found out?

Riva was fortunately none the worse for her fall. She, Hal and I were curled up in the leather chairs in the Community Archive, once again, steaming coffee cups in our hands, pondering the problem. Schultz was on my lap. I scratched him behind the ears absent-mindedly.

Noah hadn't wanted to come, fortunately. I put it down to his new interest in Jill. I felt a pang, though, as I looked at the empty chair where Mollie, eager and irrepressible, had sat during our last meeting, only a few days ago.

"Sam said that he was looking at the Machal volunteer Israeli soldier files, but that was just a bluff. Noah told us that he had never even visited Israel, let alone been a soldier. He was probably using the opportunity to find out something to his advantage; something that he could use as blackmail material," said Hal.

"But what?" said Riva.

"That we don't know, but we can look at it from another angle," said Hal. "Let's start with who was in the Community Archive at a time when Sam was here. Sam would have had to have seen what that person was reading, to make the connection. The log will tell us who was here."

"That's smart," I said.

Hal grinned. "They don't call me Vatson for nothing."

We searched the log, looking for Sam's name. He was listed twice. On the day of his first visit, four other people had also visited the Community Archive. The second time Sam had signed in, there were two others. It was possible that it was one of those six people that Sam was blackmailing.

Two of them none of us had ever heard of. They could be eliminated because they weren't residents of the Menorah. They couldn't have murdered Sam, since I hadn't noticed any outsiders in the dining room the day he died. I knew the other four. George Brody had been away visiting his children when Sam died. Sima Posner had moved out last week, so she could have had no connection to Mollie's death. Ari Gordon had since died. That left one: Pearl Green. Pearl Green?

I was so shocked that I dropped the log. "Pearl? What could she have to hide? If anyone has led a blameless life, it's Pearl," I said.

"Pearl is rich," said Riva. "Sam knew that."

I nodded. That was true. He must have realized that he could squeeze her for a lot of money, if he could find some dirt. But still... "I don't believe it," I said flatly.

"You are far too innocent, Ellie,' Riva said impatiently. "People are capable of any indignity."

"Stop squabbling," said Hal. "Let's try to find out what she was looking at."

He walked over to the shelf with the Israeli army volunteer files. "She must have been reading something near these files, if Sam was able to spy on her. This was where he was looking."

The army files were in the same row of the stacks as the local newspaper files that we had looked at before.

"Don't you remember?" I asked eagerly. "The 'Runaway Husband' columns file wasn't covered with dust, even though everything else was, and the column was half torn out. That must have been what she was looking at."

"You are right." Riva nodded. "It is possible."

"Not only possible, but probable. She was reading Libbeh's story!" said Hal, who was now as excited as I was. We were on to something. "But what on earth could there be in Libbeh's sad story that would be linked to Pearl?"

He tapped his fingers on the file, thinking. "OK, I've got an idea. What if there is some connection to Libbeh? What if Libbeh never found her missing husband but she decided to get married again anyway? What if she had children by her second husband?"

"That's a lot of 'what ifs'," I said, "but let's suppose it's all true. Why would that be material for blackmail?"

"It definitely would be," said Hal. "It would have been a disaster."

"Why would Libbeh's second marriage be a disaster for anyone?"

"Maybe it wouldn't matter to you or me, but it would matter to religious people—a lot. I'll tell you why," said Hal. "If Libbeh had given up on finding her husband, she couldn't divorce him. You can only get a divorce in Jewish law if your husband will agree to it. He has to give you what is called a *get*, in the presence of witnesses."

I thought about that. "So, if he has disappeared and can't give you a *get*, you can't get divorced?"

"You can in civil law, but not according to Jewish law. It's a big problem for Jewish women, even today. Wives in that position are called *agunot* or 'chained' women. They can't marry again."

We mulled this over. Riva had another thought. "What if Libbeh moved to another city, met someone and fell in love, and got married anyway? Suppose she pretended to be a widow, and not a deserted wife? She could have said that her first husband had died in Europe, so she didn't have a death certificate."

"That would have been an adulterous union, but there's worse. If she had children by this second, illegal marriage, they would be called *mamzers*."

I still didn't get it. "Who cares what they're called?"

"It's not just what they're called; it's what happens to them. In Jewish law, a *mamzer* is not allowed to marry a non-*mamzer* Jewish spouse. The status is hereditary too; all children of a *mamzer* are *mamzers* too. It would have implications over generations. If, say, a man were engaged to a woman and found out she was a *mamzer* in Jewish law, he wouldn't be able to marry her. A strict Orthodox rabbi would not perform the wedding."

Riva, practical as ever, had thought through the next step. "Pearl's granddaughter is engaged to a religious guy. If he found out that she was a *mamzer,* the wedding would be off. That would give Pearl a very good motive to murder Sam. She would do anything for her granddaughter—even kill the man who might prevent the wedding. But this is all just speculation. We have to find a link between Pearl and Libbeh to prove that this is true. Pearl comes from where?"

"Pearl comes from Detroit," I said. "I remember her saying that her maiden name was Melman."

"OK," said Hal. "There's a Jewish Community Archive in Detroit and we can also search marriage records to see if someone called Libbeh Cohen married a man with the last name of Melman. But I have a better idea—burial records. There are Jewish cemetery records on line. We can easily check to see if a Libbeh Melman is buried in Detroit. It will only take a few minutes... here... Yup. There's even a picture of the grave. Libbeh Melman, 1939, mourned by her husband Saul and her daughters Jennie, Sadie and... Pearl!"

We stared at one another. There was the evidence. Who would have believed it?

"That is why the page is torn," said Riva. "Pearl tried to rip it out, but when she saw that Sam was looking, she stopped. Sam was curious and after she left, looked up the page and put two and two together, just like we did."

"I wouldn't have thought that Sam was that smart," I said.

"He was shrewd. He would have to be, to be a blackmailer," said Riva. "I think he could have figured this out."

"But Pearl was shrewder," said Hal. "Fortunately, the team of Marplestein, Shoirlock and Vatson is the shrewdest of all. I think it's definitely time to tell the police what we've figured out."

I wasn't so sure. The problem was that we still hadn't figured if Pearl had actually murdered Sam. I still felt the police wouldn't believe this complicated story and I wanted to make sure that it all wasn't just a product of our fertile imaginations. I'd come this far; I wasn't going to give up now—for the sake of poor Mollie and Maurice. Yes, even for Sam, jerk that he was. I wanted to lay a trap for Pearl, but first, I had to stall Hal and Riva. The two of them would never let me do anything that they thought was dangerous.

"My head aches," I moaned. I had to get them off the subject of calling the police, at least until I had investigated further. "It's all too much. Let's go and get something to eat and think some more about it."

Hal slapped me on the back. "Right. Bring on the knishes. Tomorrow, we go to the police."

Tonight, I thought, I go to the Community Archive.

❧ Chapter Twenty-Six ❧

At dinner that evening, I set a trap. Riva had told me that she was tired, not surprisingly in view of what she had gone through, and was having dinner served to her in her room. That was a bit of luck for me. She would have been horrified if she had known what I had in mind.

"I hear there's been progress in the murder case," I said casually to Pearl and Bernice.

"What murder case?" asked Pearl. "I thought the police decided that Sam died of a heart attack and Maurice was locked in the freezer by mistake. Now they think they were murdered?"

"Maurice was murdered?" asked her faithful sidekick, Bernice, only a few beats behind.

For once, I didn't deny it. "I heard from Ms. Robins that they found some evidence in the Community Archive and they're sending a team to investigate in the morning. I may have a look myself tonight."

Pearl ate her dinner thoughtfully. She seemed to have nothing more to say. Aha. The trap was baited.

But then, I had second thoughts. Was I crazy taking my chances in a deserted building with a woman who might well be a murderer? What if Pearl turned up tonight, as I figured she would, and then saw me? She would have nothing to lose by killing me too. What was one corpse, more or less?

If I told Hal or Riva or even worse, Josh, what I planned, though, in the hopes that they would come along, they would never let me go. Hal might say that he was working on not being bossy, but I knew that was just talk. He wasn't going to change—not at his age. And as for Riva, she would just bully me into leaving it to the police. No, this was a job for Shoirlick, without the aid of Vatson and Miss Marplestein. I had to do this job by myself. Neither of them could know anything about it.

Riva and Hal trusted the police, but I didn't. I knew Detective Smyth and Lieutenant Johnson too well. The idea of describing what a *get* or an *agunah* was to that cynical pair, let alone explaining why those abstruse Jewish legal terms could provide a motive for murder, was mind-boggling. They already thought I was nuts. This would just reinforce their opinion.

But on the other hand... I didn't really want to go alone. Jeez... it was scary! Who else could I count on? There was Noah, but he was just a kid. I couldn't put him in danger. What I could do though, was have him on standby. I could tell him that if I didn't return by a certain time, he should call Hal. And then there was Schultz. Ok, he was a dog, but he was a smart dog. He could bite. And with Riva recovering from her fall, I was looking after him anyway, so there was no problem taking him along without anybody knowing.

Of course, if anything happened to Schultz, I wouldn't need Pearl to murder me. Riva would gladly do the job herself. I would have to take that chance; Schultz would be company and I needed company.

At 8 that evening, I called on Sam's family, the Levins, who were due to leave next day. They were just finishing packing up, and the apartment looked sadly impersonal, with the last few boxes strewn over the living room floor. They had offered most of Sam's belongings to staff members who had been happy to take them; I had seen George schlepping the painting on velvet of the green-faced lady to his car.

"I just wanted to say good-bye," I said to Joy, Sam's daughter-in-law.

"Thanks for coming by," she said warmly. "And thanks for being so nice to Noah. Not everyone wants to spend time with a teenager, but you did. We're grateful." Milton shook my hand. "We're leaving in the morning. It's been difficult, but I think we've sorted everything out."

"Is Noah around? I'd like to say good-bye to him too."

"Sure. He's in the bedroom, with Jill. They've become good friends over the past few days," said Joy.

Noah and Jill looked like more than good friends, when I opened the door of the bedroom. They sprung apart. Jill looked embarrassed; Noah preened, as well he might. Jill was a pretty classy girlfriend for a shnook like him. I was glad that he realized how lucky he was. She would be good for him in a lot of ways, assuming they found a way to be together.

"Noah and Jill, I want to say good-bye and thanks for all your help, but I also want to ask for a favor," I said.

"Sure. Whadda you want us to do? Sneak a peek at Zaidie's computer again? I bet he was watching pornography—I could find it."

Jill gave him a sharp look. "You don't look at pornography, do you? It demeans women."

"Who, me? Nah," said Noah, turning red.

We were getting off the subject here. "No, what I want you to do is sit in the lobby tonight. I'm planning to go to the Archive to see what clues I can find. It may be that someone will follow me. Keep an eye on who goes out, and if I don't get back by midnight, call Hal and tell him where I am. Can you do that?"

"Sure," said Jill. "Is it dangerous?"

Noah perked up. "Dangerous? Can I come with you? Jill can sit in the lobby and check things out."

"No! I'm taking Schultz with me, so I don't need you. I'll have my inhaler just in case my asthma acts up. Anyway, it's not dangerous."

"I'll see you two then at 11 o'clock tonight in the lobby."

Sure enough, Jill and Noah were waiting for me in the lobby, when I came down with Schultz at 11. Naturally, the place was deserted. Eleven o'clock was the middle of the night for most of the residents of the Menorah. Even Josh had retired early, perhaps worn out by all the yoga exercises. That was good news for me, since I could easily sneak past him without waking him up, and without worrying that he would come home and find me missing.

"Has anyone gone out?" I asked them.

"Nope, nobody," said Noah. He and Jill were both texting on their cell phones. Could they possibly be texting each other on their phones, even though they were sitting right next to one another? What a world.

I had gotten the key to the Community Archive by a ruse: I had borrowed Hal's extra key on the grounds that I wanted to check something on the day that he didn't work there. He hadn't suspected a thing. Then I had "forgotten" to return the key. Pretty sneaky, eh? I was turning into a great detective. Or maybe a criminal. Or both. This was getting confusing.

It was dark and cold, a moonless night with very little visibility, but at least it wasn't snowing for a change. Schultz didn't seem too eager to go for a stroll at this time of night, but I kicked him gently on the rear.

"Move, boy. We've got a job to do." He whined. It was obvious he was eager to get back to Riva, who never did nutty things like this. It was cold outside.

The Community Archive was even darker inside than it was outside, but I didn't turn on any lights. I'll just sit here in the dark, I thought. It was like the punch line of a joke. The time passed slowly. I yawned...

Schultz's low growl woke me up. Drat.. half an hour had passed while I was dozing. The door was open and the hall light was on, which it hadn't been before. And the key to the Community Archive, which had been on the desk beside me, was gone. This was ominous. There was someone here in the Community Archive with me; someone who had taken the key. I felt a chill that had nothing to do with the temperature.

"Hello?" I called. My voice quavered. Not surprisingly, there was no answer. Fortunately, I had Schultz, my own private guard with me.

"Who's here, Schultz?"

The dog wagged his tail and trotted off towards the stacks. I followed, cautiously. A thick book, hurled from the shadowy end of the row of shelves, hit me on the shoulder, barely missing my head.

"Ow!" I rubbed my shoulder. Another book, thrown with less energy, landed at my feet, which gave me some encouragement. The intruder seemed to be running out of steam. Anyway, if his or her best weapon was a book, I could deal with it. I ran forward, and tripped over a third book that I hadn't seen in the gloom, landing hard on the floor and knocking my breath out. Before I could recover, a figure loomed over me. It was Pearl.

I was right! Pearl was the killer. She had taken the bait and come to the Community Archive to stop me finding out something that would implicate her—something that I had already pieced together. Somehow, though, proving that I had been right didn't provide much consolation in the predicament I found myself in. Boy, I had been dumb not to take someone with me. Even Smyth and Johnson would have been welcome at this point.

"Why didn't you mind your own business, Ellie?" Pearl asked. She sounded sad rather than angry. Maybe she didn't like to knock off her friends. I was somewhat relieved to see that she wasn't holding a knife, or even a book. Maybe I could play dumb and extricate myself.

"Hi, Pearl. What are you doing here? Did you feel like finding something to read too?" I asked brightly.

"I'm not an idiot, Ellie. It's not Bernice you're talking to. I know you've figured out what I was after. Well, here it is."

She thrust a handful of torn newspaper pages in front of my face. Of course, they were the pages of the newspaper with Libbeh's story. The story of her mother.

"Do you think you can stop my granddaughter Sarah from getting married? Well, you can't. Nobody can. Sam thought he could blackmail me when he found out, but you saw what happened to him."

Even in the shadowy light that came from the hall, Pearl looked determined and beyond reason. I had no doubt that she meant what she said.

"How did you do it, Pearl? How did you manage to get the pills into the knish?"

She looked pleased with herself. "Oh, you figured out that the knishes were stuffed with pills? Well, I didn't do it. Bernice did. She wants to be my friend so badly that she does everything I tell her and she doesn't have a clue why she's actually doing it. She just says that she's going to the bathroom, and nobody doubts it or notices what she's doing.

"I knew Sam was taking medicine for a heart condition and that he was drinking. That would be a lethal combination with the pills. I told Bernice that Sam needed the pill for his condition and she should slip a couple of pills into his knish on her way to the bathroom.

"Do you remember that she stumbled when she was near his table, and pulled herself up with the tablecloth? That's when she did it. No one noticed, but if someone had noticed, I would just have said that she didn't know what she was doing. Everyone knows that she's half out of her mind. Even if she said that she had done it, no one would have believed her. But in any case, everyone was so busy watching Sam perform that no one noticed. I bet you didn't either, did you?"

She was right. I hadn't.

Maybe flattery would work and get me out of here. "That was very clever, Pearl. How did you manage with Maurice?"

"Same thing. He was suspicious because he overheard Sam demanding money from me, so I told Bernice to pretend to go to the bathroom, make sure Maurice was alone in the kitchen, then ask for something from the freezer and close the door with him inside. It worked beautifully."

"Wow. There's no stopping you, is there? You smothered Mollie, didn't you? And you waxed the leg tips of Riva's walker."

"Of course. Mollie was too inquisitive. Sooner or later, she would have seen something suspicious. Then, when she joined up with you and Riva, I knew she had to go. It was easy enough to smother her. And Riva? I hate her. She thinks she's better than anybody, because she survived the Holocaust. Well, she almost didn't survive this. Like you won't."

I wanted to get up and stop her, but I had begun to wheeze. I was having trouble catching my breath. Where was my inhaler?

Pearl walked over to my bag, which had fallen on the floor, and pulled out my inhaler. Then she tossed it in the wastepaper basket. "You won't be needing this anymore," she said.

Then she pulled a book of matches from her pocket, lit one and held the flame to the newspaper fragments that she was holding. The flickering flame was reflected in her wild, desperate eyes. She held the burning paper until the black ashes curled to her fingers, and then she dropped it on the floor, still smoldering. I was paralyzed with fright and wheezing too heavily to attempt to stop her.

"That's the last time anyone reads the story of my poor mother and what she suffered. Good-bye Ellie. We won't be meeting again,"

She tossed another lit match into the library stacks and then walked quickly to the door, aiming a kick at Schultz on the way. So much for his help, the useless mutt. I heard the key turn in the lock and then the crackling of flames. The embers from the old, dry newspaper clippings had set a pile of files on the floor on fire, and they were beginning to flicker. The Community Archive was on fire, and I was locked in.

Help! What had I done?

❧ Chapter Twenty-Seven ❧

To my horror, I saw the files on the floor smoldering. The smoke grew thicker and the smoke alarm began to whine. Pearl's match had set the newspapers on fire and I wondered how long it would be before the files all burst into flame. Not long, for sure; piled to the ceiling with books and papers, the Community Archive was a pyromaniac's dream.

Pearl had locked the door so that I couldn't get out, but she had made the mistake of underestimating me and not tying me up. No doubt she thought that an asthma attack would keep me incapacitated until the fire did me in. On the floor, I was paralyzed with fright, but I realized one thing: I needed my inhaler, fast. Fortunately, Pearl had tossed it in the wastepaper basket, not out the window. I crawled over, retrieved it and used it. That was better. I felt much stronger.

It was now past midnight. If Noah and Jill had done what I asked them to do and alerted Hal, help might be on the way. Unfortunately, right now there was no sign of anyone. I would have to pull myself together and do something, unless I wanted to end up fried like a blintz. Beside me, Schultz whimpered. He didn't like the situation any better than I did, the coward.

"You could have defended me," I said to him. "You weren't much use." His tail between his legs, Schultz looked ashamed of himself, confirming my suspicion that he understood everything.

Not that it did either of us any good.

But scolding the dog wasn't much use either. What to do? I looked around frantically.

Water! The kitchenette! With some effort, I pulled myself up from the floor, hobbled to the kitchen and filled the coffee pot with water, which I poured on the burning files. A few more trips back and forth for pots of water, and the flames died out. Then I smothered the remaining embers with a throw rug.

Ok, that wasn't so bad. There was lots of smoke, but very little damage. Schultz and I were still alive and kicking. Well, alive anyway. I rubbed my aching back. I wouldn't be doing any kicking any time soon.

I opened a window to disperse the smoke and peered out. Yes! There, in the distance and heading towards the Community Archive, was my pal, Hal. And there also was Pearl, who had just left the building and was heading in the opposite direction, towards the entrance of the Menorah. Their paths crossed. Would Hal stop her?

I leaned out of the window so he could see me and stabbed my finger in the direction of Pearl—"get her!"—but Hal shook his head, clearly influenced by the smoke pouring from the window. Pearl ran past him and Hal made no move to stop her. It was obvious he had decided that his first priority was me.

Pearl had locked the door to the Community Archive so that I couldn't get out, but that didn't stop Hal from getting in. Of course, I remembered, he had his own key.

"Are you all right?" He coughed as he ran into the room, waving away the smoke, and looked at me intently.

"I'm fine," I said, shrugging off his arm. "Don't worry about me. We have to catch Pearl."

"Catch her?" Hal looked bewildered.

"Have you forgotten? I know for sure now that our assumption was right. She's the killer."

Hal shook his head. "We don't really know for sure. We were just guessing. Are you positive you're not jumping to conclusions again?"

"Pearl definitely killed Sam, Maurice and Mollie," I said. "I'll tell you all about it later. Right now we have to stop her. She's gone back to the Menorah and I don't trust her." I was frantically trying to persuade him, but he wasn't buying it.

"Relax. We can call the police," Hal said.

"Oh Hal," I said impatiently. Would he never take me seriously?

I didn't have time for this. Pushing him aside, I ran past him into the winter night, with Schultz barking at my heels. I hadn't bothered with my coat, and the icy wind whipped my hair and caught in my lungs. For about the thousandth time, I wondered why on earth I had chosen to live in Minnesota and not, say, Hawaii.

Hal followed, but glancing back, I saw that he had slipped on the icy path and fallen. I couldn't wait for him. He didn't seem hurt; in fact he was slowly standing up. I figured he could catch up with me.

Where was Pearl? I couldn't see her, so she must have gone into the building. If Jill and Noah had any sense, they would put two and two together and try to stop her. But did they have any sense?

For once, they did.

As I stumbled into the thankfully warm entrance hall, I saw Jill tugging at Pearl by the sleeve of her sweater. Pearl pulled away.

"Pearl!" I yelled.

She gaped as if she couldn't believe what she was seeing. I could understand that; the last time she had seen me, I was lying on the floor of a room she was about to lock, with a pile of dry newspaper files smoldering beside me. She must have thought Schultz and I had come back from the dead.

Pearl looked frantic. It was clear that her options were limited. She could run back outside, but what then? She had no transport, no money, no resources. That meant she would have to find some means of escape inside the Menorah. But where? The entrance to the Vintage Coffee House was on the left; Ms. Robins' office on the right. Neither were of much use to Pearl. But there, at the back of the entrance hall was the curved grand staircase leading up to the mezzanine library. That was where she headed.

I had no idea what she would do when she got to the library, and I imagined that she didn't either, but she was cornered and desperate. There was no other choice.

As I followed her, with Noah, Jill and Schultz behind me, I thought back to all the drama that had happened in the library—Sam's *shiva;* Mollie's *shiva;* the computer revelations. Would there be more drama? How would it end?

I heard a siren in the distance. Someone had evidently called the police; probably Hal. Good. For once, I wouldn't be sorry to see Lieutenant Johnson and Detective Smyth.

At the top of the stairs, Pearl halted, clearly uncertain what to do. The mezzanine floor had a wrought iron railing around it on the side that was open to the entrance hall below and from that vantage point, she could see everyone entering the building. What she saw from her point of view was not good. Hal had come into the building, and Jill, Noah and I were right behind her. Even Josh, in pajamas, was bringing up the rear.

It was spunky little Schultz who was the first to reach Pearl. He growled and nipped at her foot. In a fury, she picked him up. He barked and tried to wiggle out of her grasp.

"Let him go, Pearl. He can't do you any harm," I yelled.

But Schultz seemed a symbol to Pearl of a hateful world which only wanted to spoil her granddaughter's happiness. She raised the little terrier over her head and then hurled him with all her strength over the railing. To my horror, I watched as Schultz, yipping pitifully, sailed through the air in a wide arc and disappeared from view. Then—a dull thud. I screwed my eyes; I couldn't look.

"Did you have to do that?" I asked sadly.

Pearl spoke to me for the first time since we had reached the Menorah.

"That stupid dog. I'm glad to see the last of him."

"Please, Pearl, give up," I pleaded, as I edged towards her. "You'll get off easily."

"How did you get out of the Archive, Ellie?" she sobbed. "I set it on fire. Why aren't you dead? You have to die too, so the police won't know that I killed Sam."

Pearl wasn't making a whole lot of sense, but she seemed to have lost touch with reality. All that mattered to her was that no one should stop the marriage of her beloved granddaughter Sarah.

Tears were running down her cheeks now. "Sam tried to ruin Sarah's life. He deserved to die. Why did you have to interfere, Ellie? I didn't want to hurt you."

We were both standing at the railing at the top of the stairs now. There was a sudden blur of movement. A little terrier was racing towards Pearl, teeth bared. Schultz had survived his fall.

"Schultz! You're alive," I cried.

Not only was he alive, but he looked really, really pissed.

Heading straight for his nemesis, he bit Pearl's ankle. Pearl shrieked and toppled over backwards. She bumped down the stairs, head first, until, to my horror, she lay ominously still at the bottom. There was no doubt in my mind that she would do no more, ever, for her granddaughter.

∾ ∾

Once again, Hal and I were sitting in my living room, enjoying cups of tea and generous pieces of chocolate yeast babka. To my surprise and delight, he wasn't angry with me, even though I hadn't told him beforehand about my secret plan to wait for Pearl in the Community Archive. (Josh was another story; he was furious.)

My asthma attack had passed off, thanks to the inhaler, and in spite of a lingering regret and sadness about what Pearl had done and her horrifying death, I felt at peace.

"I've done trying to boss you around," Hal said.

I was pleased to hear that. "You've learned that I'm smart enough to take care of myself."

"No. I've learned that it's hopeless trying to tell you anything," he said, wincing. He had bruised his hip when he fell outside, but thankfully, suffered no serious damage.

"Fill in the blanks for me," I urged. "First of all, how did Schultz survive?"

"He fell onto Mollie's sofa. It broke his fall. You'd almost think that Mollie had a hand in saving him."

Maybe she did, I thought. I had a mental image of Mollie, in her Nancy Drewski costume, sitting on the sofa with her arms stretched to catch Schultz.

"And what about Maurice? Pearl told me that she ordered Bernice to try and get him to fetch something from the freezer and then shut the door on him. Do you think Bernice knew what she was doing?"

"Who knows? Anyway, her family has decided that she needs more care than she's getting at the Menorah, so they're moving her to another facility with more supervision. And do you know what? She's stopped going to the bathroom so often. I suspect that Pearl may have been giving her a diuretic."

There was one thing I still had to know.

"How much of Pearl's story do the police know?"

Hal hesitated. "I haven't told them anything. I think it's best that they assume that she went a little crazy and just fell down the stairs. I wouldn't want to stop her granddaughter's marriage. What the fiancé doesn't know won't hurt him. If we don't say anything, no one will ever know that the wedding was almost prevented. I think that it will only do harm if we tell the truth. What do you think?"

"I absolutely agree," I said firmly. "For the sake of her granddaughter, let the police think that Sam, Maurice and Mollie died naturally. It will be our secret."

"Our secret. Ours and Libbeh's."

He smiled and took my hand. I felt dizzy with happiness. Could this actually be happening, to me, Ellie?

Hal cleared his throat nervously. "There's something else I want to say. You're a very special person, Ellie. Not too many women would have tolerated the way I behaved to you. I never stopped criticizing and you've put up with it like a saint. Well, most of the time.

"I've grown to respect and" he cleared his throat. "...well, to care for you, Ellie. Could you feel the same? We're still in our 70s—we might have 10, maybe even 20 good years ahead of us, with luck. We don't have to get married, but we could be together."

He looked at me anxiously.

I hadn't seen this coming. A few weeks ago, this scenario would have been wonderful beyond my wildest dreams. I wouldn't have hesitated for a second. But things had changed. How could I explain this, without hurting Hal?

I took a deep breath. This was going to be hard, but I had to try.

"Hal, I grew up with domineering parents, married an overbearing husband and had two children who still think they know better than I do. All my life, I've deferred to other people. It's taken me more than 70 years to grow up, but I've finally done it. Trying to solve the murder of Sam helped me prove to myself that I have the gumption to accomplish things on my own. And I like the feeling. Of course I want to be with you, but I want some time to be on my own as well. I think we should continue the way we are."

Hal smiled, a little wryly. "I'll take what I can get."

He took my hand and the expression in his eyes overwhelmed me. It beat, I had to admit, even knishes.

❧ Chapter Twenty-Eight ❦

Spring had come, the garden was in bloom and there were fragrant lilacs, my favorite flower, on the tables in the Menorah dining room. The occasion was the monthly party for all the residents who were celebrating a birthday that month. This time, there were 15 birthdays. Streamers and balloons fluttered from the chandelier of the dining room and the new maitre d', Orlando, beaming, was now wheeling in a cake on a trolley.

The three-layered apple cake looked darn good, I thought. It had taken me two days to get right, particularly since I had given in to Dolly's non-negotiable demand about using whole wheat flour in everything I baked. I had agreed because, in fact, the healthy cookies she had baked in my suite had turned out not half bad.

Orlando lit the candles, the birthday girls and boys blew them out, and waiters began distributing pieces of cake to the tables.

"What a beautiful cake!" said Hindy.

Riva and I now had two new women sitting at our table in place of Pearl and Bernice. One was Hindy, a pleasant woman in her 80s, who was new to the Menorah. The other, unfortunately, was Joyce, who had moved back. In fact, most of the residents who had moved out during the panic about Sam and Maurice had changed their minds and sheepishly returned. The truth was, the Menorah was still a cut above all the other retirement homes in the area and everybody knew it.

The atmosphere was so upbeat these days that there was talk of producing a nude calendar featuring the residents. Riva had had plenty to say about that, though a surprising number of women were keen to be part of the project. Hal teased me that I should be one of them. In his dreams.

Without Mollie to spread the gossip, the general feeling was that Sam had died of a heart attack, Maurice was the inadvertent victim of an accident, Mollie had passed away peacefully in her sleep and Pearl, well, Pearl had slipped and fallen. We hadn't enlightened anyone. I had heard that her granddaughter's wedding had been one of the fanciest the town had seen in a long time.

Joyce, unfortunately, was still Joyce, though she was now best buddies with Dolly. The two of them had bonded over the horrors of unhealthy food. They had even persuaded Tommy to cook more broccoli and cauliflower. The new vegetable regime wasn't popular with residents—they claimed it gave them gas—and I couldn't see it lasting.

"Dolly told me that apple cake gives you diabetes," she said, as usual spoiling the occasion.

Riva rolled her eyes and deliberately took a big bite.

"Oh, did you make the cake, Ellie?" Joyce asked.

"Yes," I said shortly.

"Did you put artificial sweetener in it, instead of sugar, so we wouldn't get diabetes? Oh, no" she reminded herself. "Dolly said that artificial sweeteners give you cancer."

"Don't eat the cake, Joyce, if you are worried." Riva's spill on the ice hadn't affected her tart tongue or made her any more tactful, but her manner didn't intimidate me anymore. On the contrary, I felt I'd gained a best friend during the course of our adventure.

"You made the cake? It's wonderful," said Hindy, who was clearly going to be a great improvement on Pearl and Bernice.

"I'm glad you like it. In fact, I made two cakes," I said. "This one and a small one for Noah, to thank him for all his help. He came for a visit with his parents last week, to finish settling up his grandfather's affairs, and also, I think, to visit Jill. You never met Noah, Hindy, but he was the grandson of a fellow who used to live here."

(I had actually made three; one for Hal too, but there was no need to go into that.)

"Did Noah have the good manners to thank you?" asked Riva, looking skeptical.

"Yes, actually he did, and he even gave me a hug. His mother looked astonished. I think Jill has civilized him a little."

"I think it is more likely that I civilized him a little," said Riva. She was probably right.

Ms. Robins strode into the dining room, and came over to our table, all smiles. I knew she had noticed Schultz under the table licking up the cake crumbs—a definite no-no—but she said nothing. In fact she winked at me. There was no doubt about it. Ms. Robins had changed.

No longer nervous about her job since the deserters had returned, and free of worry about blackmail, she was far more relaxed and easy-going. The wig had disappeared and she now had a new short, curly hairstyle. She was even wearing pants. They looked good on her. I thought her behind looked quite pinchable these days, and I hoped she would meet someone who thought so too.

She had brought her son Jamie to a few events at the Menorah. "I'm tired of hiding," she had told me. "I'm not ashamed of my son, so let everyone meet him."

And we had. To her delight, Jamie had been a hit. Far from seeing his disability as something to be ashamed of, the residents had welcomed him. His charm and good nature had made him popular with everyone, and having a son like Jamie had humanized Ms. Robins in their eyes. Jamie loved coming to the Menorah too and had made friends with many people. He especially loved Schultz, who loved him back. On my part, I had started teaching him to bake (Jamie, that is, not Schultz.)

"Hi girls," said Ms. Robins, pulling up a spare chair and joining us at the table. "I see you're enjoying Ellie's apple cake."

"Yes," said Riva. "It is not bad."

Well, that was Riva. Compliments from her were rare, although, to be fair, you always got the truth. I preferred that to false praise. Actually I preferred any kind of praise at all, true or false, but I had gotten used to the fact that I wasn't going to get much of it from Riva. That was ok; to my delight, I was getting lots of praise these days. Some of it was for my baking, and some for my romance with Hal, a hot topic of gossip which had raised my status in everyone's estimation. That was ok too.

"I think the cake is more than just not bad," said Ms. Robins—Justine, as she now insisted we call her. "Ellie's baking is excellent, as usual."

"It's given me my ample figure," I said, remembering what Ms. Robins had once told me.

"Ample? Nonsense. I would say voluptuous," she said. I let it pass. If she wanted to be friends, that was fine with me.

But now, she changed the subject, "Has Ellie told you our news?"

Three quizzical faces looked at me. "What news?" asked Riva. "You are getting married, Ellie?" She looked alarmed. Thank God for small mercies—at least Pearl and Bernice weren't around to hear this fascinating bit of phony gossip.

"No, of course not. It's just that the Menorah management has asked me to develop a small catering business. I'll be directing a team of bakers and cooks producing a line of traditional Jewish food—latkes at Hanukah, honey cakes at the New Year, challah breads on the Sabbath, and so on. Knishes too, of course. We're going to sell them to the public, and maybe, if it all works, expand to other outlets. I've already had an order for rugelach from Lieutenant Johnson and Detective Smyth."

I couldn't help feeling gratified. In all my life, I'd never faced such a challenge and when I had told the children, instead of putting me down, they had cheered me on. Josh had even said he was proud of me. That was a first in my life.

Perhaps he had learned something from Ms Gold, who had also asked me to call her by her first name, Shayna. I was beginning to think that Josh was dragging out his visits to the Menorah not on my account, but because of Shayna. The two of them had been spending a lot of time together, and I had never seen Josh so enraptured. It was amusing to think of my practical son meditating, or earth mother Shayna driving his Porsche, but hey, whatever worked. I was delighted. I was sure Shayna would want lots of kids.

Justine put her arm around me. "We're going to employ a few people with disabilities to do simple jobs in the kitchen too, including Jamie. He's over the moon about having another regular job. And we have Ellie to thank for it all."

Riva cleared her throat.

"Riva too, of course," she amended. "And Hal and Schultz. Even Noah."

Once again, an indistinct image of Mollie floated into my mind. Wearing her brightest muu-muu, red lipstick and thick mascara, she was hovering over her sofa like a character in a Chagall painting Or could that be Libbeh, floating above Popoisk? In my mind, I saw Mollie/Libbeh toss a knish in the air and catch it with a flourish. She winked at me.

Maybe, I thought, we also have to thank Mollie and Libbeh. I winked back.

THE END

✒ Ellie's Recipes ❧

Knishes

1 cup flour
Pinch salt
1 tsp baking power

Mix. Make well. Add following three ingredients:

¼ cup oil
1 egg
1 tsp vinegar plus enough hot water to make up ¼ cup

Mix with wooden spoon and form into ball. Chill for half an hour.

Mash *two boiled potatoes and mix with 1 pkg onion soup and one egg.*

Roll out dough to rectangle, put potato mixture along one edge and roll up. Cut into pieces and form into knish shapes. Bake until light brown—about 10 minutes.

Cottage Cheese Muffins

2 cartons creamed cottage cheese (500 gr)
2 tsp sugar
4 eggs
3 cups flour
½ cup melted butter
Salt
3 tsp baking powder
1 cup cheddar cheese
½ cup milk
100 grams goat cheese, melted with the butter

Mix. Place in greased muffin tins. Bake at 400 degrees for 15-20 minutes.

Mandelbroit

2 cups flour
½ tsp baking soda
1 tsp baking powder
Salt
4 oz butter
Zest of 1 lemon
¾ cup sugar
Tsp vanilla
2 eggs
1 cup chopped walnuts or almonds

Cream butter and sugar. Add eggs, vanilla and zest. Mix flour, baking soda, salt, baking powder and add to mixture. Add flour slowly and then nuts. Form into roll about 2 inches wide. Bake at 350 degrees for about 15 minutes. Take out of oven, cool, cut diagonally into slices and put each slice back in oven until lightly brown. Turn over and bake the other side 5 minutes.

Rugelach

2 cups flour
1/4 teaspoon salt
¼ cup sugar
1 pkg (8 oz) cold cream cheese
1 cup butter
1 tsp vanilla

Combine flour, sugar and salt. In food processor, place flour mixture, cream cheese and butter and process until like crumbs. Mix in vanilla. Form into 4 balls and chill for at least an hour. Roll out into circles. Sprinkle with mixture of ½ cup brown sugar, ½ cup white sugar, 1 tsp cinnamon, 1 cup chopped nuts. Slice dough into 12 wedges. Roll up, thick end first. Bake on parchment paper on baking trays until golden brown, about 15 minutes.

Potato Kugel

5 medium potatoes, grated and peeled (can use food processor)
1 large onion, grated
3 eggs
2 tbs vegetable oil
1 tsp salt
½ tsp pepper

Grease a 9 x 12 inch pan with oil, combine rest of ingredients and pour into pan. Drizzle top with 1 tbsp oil. Bake until golden brown on top at 180 degrees C—about ½ hour.

Cheese Blintzes

Crepes

2 eggs
½ cup milk
½ cup flour, or enough to make a cream-like mixture
Pinch salt
1 tsp oil
1 Tbsp sugar

Filling

8 oz farmer cheese or cream cheese
¼ cup sugar
1 Tbsp flour
1 tsp lemon juice
1 egg yolk
(optional) ½ cup raisins

For crepes, combine eggs, milk and blend. Gradually add flour, then sugar, salt and oil. Beat well. (This can be done in food processor.) Let rest for half an hour.

For filling, combine all ingredients in a bowl and beat well.

Fry crepes: Using a paper towel or brush, apply a thin coating of oil to a 7 inch skillet. Ladle approximately 1/3 cup of batter into the skillet. Tilt pan so batter covers the bottom of the skillet. Fry on one side until top is set. Carefully loosen edges of crepe with pancake turner and slide onto a plate or towel. Repeat until batter is used up. Place 2 tablespoons of filling on edge of crepe, fried side up, and roll into envelope shape. When all the filling is used up, fry the blintzes until golden brown.

Apple Strudel

4 medium size apples
½ cup sugar
½ tsp salt
1 tsp cinnamon
1 tbsp flour
100 gr butter (1 stick) melted
Eight sheets thawed filo dough, covered with damp towel.

Peel and core; slice thinly about ¼ inch and cut in half. Add sugar, cinnamon, flour and tsp salt. Mix together. Melt butter. Brush 4 sheets filo dough with butter, add apple filling. Place remaining sheet on top and brush with more butter. Roll up carefully on sheet of baking paper. Brush top with butter. Sprinkle with 1 tbsp sugar. Bake until brown and apples are soft, about half an hour. Slice.

Lokshen (Home-Made Noodles)

Start with about 2 ½ *cups of flour* (You may need more.). Add ½ *tsp salt* and mix. Place flour on board or slab and make a well in center. Add *2 eggs*. You can use your hand or a wooden spoon to incorporate the eggs and form a soft dough. If more flour is needed, add as required. Knead well. Rest the dough for at least an hour, then, on a large surface, such as a table covered with a cloth, roll out with a rolling pin and then stretch the dough as thinly as possible. Roll it up and cut into strips. Let the dough rest for another hour or so. Drop into boiling salted water or soup and cook for about five minutes.

Apple Cake

First peel and cut *5 or 6 apples* into square chunks about the size of a thimble. Sprinkle in *2 tbsp cinnamon* and *5 tbsp sugar* and set aside. Into a large bowl, measure:

3 cups flour (whole wheat or regular)
2 cups sugar
1 cup oil
4 eggs
½ cup orange juice
3 tsp baking powder
2 ½ tsp vanilla
1 tsp salt

Beat these together until smooth and pour half the batter into bundt pan. Arrange half the apple mixture on top. Pour in remaining batter and top with apple. Place in preheated 350 degree oven and bake about 1 ½ hours or until done.

A NOTE TO READERS

If you enjoyed this book, I would be most grateful if you would consider posting a review on the retailer website where you purchased the book, Goodreads, or any other reader site or blog you frequent.

ALSO BY CAROL NOVIS

"Tension on a Pension" Mysteries

Long in the Sleuth

Knock Off the Old Block (coming 2017)

Children's Books

The Adventures of Mary Fairy

ABOUT THE AUTHOR

Born in Winnipeg, Canada, Carol Novis is a journalist and editor who has worked for newspapers and magazines in Canada, the US, South Africa and Israel. Now living in Israel, she writes fiction, including the children's book *The Adventures of Mary Fairy,* and like her heroine Ellie, enjoys baking. Other interests include reading, walking, travel and her grandchildren. The next book in the "Tension on a Pension" mystery series, *Knock Off the Old Block,* is due to be released late in 2017.

Connect at: carolnovis.com; on Facebook (www.facebook.com/sleuthcozymystery); and at Goodreads.

Made in the USA
Middletown, DE
22 January 2018